NASHVILLE – BOOK THREE – WHAT WE FEEL

INGLATH COOPER

Contents

Copyright	vii
Books by Inglath Cooper	ix
Reviews	xi
CeCe	1
Holden	11
CeCe	19
Holden	31
CeCe	39
Holden	45
CeCe	51
Holden	59
CeCe	63
CeCe	75
CeCe	81
Holden	87
CeCe	91
CeCe	97
Nashville – Book Four – Pleasure in the Rain	103
Books by Inglath Cooper	105
	107
About Inglath Cooper	109

Copyright

Books by Inglath Cooper

My Italian Lover – What If – Book One
Fences
Dragonfly Summer – Book Two – Smith Mountain Lake Series
Blue Wide Sky – Book One – Smith Mountain Lake Series
That Month in Tuscany
Crossing Tinker's Knob
Jane Austen Girl
Good Guys Love Dogs
Truths and Roses
Nashville – Book Ten – Not Without You
Nashville – Book Nine – You, Me and a Palm Tree
Nashville – Book Eight – R U Serious
Nashville – Book Seven – Commit
Nashville – Book Six – Sweet Tea and Me
Nashville – Book Five – Amazed
Nashville – Book Four – Pleasure in the Rain
Nashville – Book Three – What We Feel
Nashville – Book Two – Hammer and a Song
Nashville – Book One – Ready to Reach
On Angel's Wings
A Gift of Grace
RITA® Award Winner John Riley's Girl
A Woman With Secrets
Unfinished Business
A Woman Like Annie
The Lost Daughter of Pigeon Hollow
A Year and a Day

Reviews

"If you like your romance in New Adult flavor, with plenty of ups and downs, oh-my, oh-yes, oh-no, love at first sight, trouble, happiness, difficulty, and follow-your-dreams, look no further than extraordinary prolific author Inglath Cooper. Ms. Cooper understands that the romance genre deserves good writing, great characterization, and true-to-life settings and situations, no matter the setting. I recommend you turn off the phone and ignore the doorbell, as you're not going to want to miss a moment of this saga of the girl who headed for Nashville with only a guitar, a hound, and a Dream in her heart." – Mallory Heart Reviews

"Truths and Roses . . . so sweet and adorable, I didn't want to stop reading it. I could have put it down and picked it up again in the morning, but I didn't want to." – Kirkusreviews.com

On Truths and Roses: "I adored this book…what romance should be, entwined with real feelings, real life and roses blooming. Hats off to the author, best book I have read in a while." – Rachel Dove, FrustratedYukkyMommyBlog

"I am a sucker for sweet love stories! This is definitely one of those! It was a very easy, well written, book. It was easy to follow, detailed, and didn't leave me hanging without answers." – www.layfieldbaby.blogspot.com

"I don't give it often, but I am giving it here – the sacred 10. Why? Inglath Cooper's A GIFT OF GRACE mesmerized me; I consumed it in one sitting. When I turned the last page, it was three in the morning." – MaryGrace Meloche, Contemporary Romance Writers

5 Blue Ribbon Rating! ". . .More a work of art than a story. . .Tragedies affect entire families as well as close loved ones, and this story portrays that beautifully as well as giving the reader hope that somewhere out there is A GIFT OF GRACE for all of us." — Chrissy Dionne, Romance Junkies 5 Stars

"A warm contemporary family drama, starring likable people coping with tragedy and triumph." 4 1/2 Stars. — Harriet Klausner

"A GIFT OF GRACE is a beautiful, intense, and superbly written novel about grief and letting go, second chances and coming alive again after devastating adversity. Warning!! A GIFT OF GRACE is a three-hanky read...better make that a BIG box of tissues read! Wowsers, I haven't cried so much while reading a book in a long long time...Ms. Cooper's skill makes A GIFT OF GRACE totally believable, totally absorbing...and makes Laney Tucker vibrantly alive. This book will get into your heart and it will NOT let go. A GIFT OF GRACE is simply stunning in every way—brava, Ms. Cooper! Highly, highly recommended!" – 4 1/2 Hearts — Romance Readers Connection

"...A WOMAN WITH SECRETS...a powerful love story laced with treachery, deceit and old wounds that will not heal...enchanting tale...weaved with passion, humor, broken hearts and a commanding love that will have your heart soaring and cheering for a happily-ever-after love. Kate is strong-willed, passionate and suffers a bruised heart. Cole is sexy, stubborn and also suffers a bruised heart...gripping plot. I look forward to reading more of Ms. Cooper's work!" – www.freshfiction.com

CeCe

19 months later

The Blue Bird is packed for the early show. Thomas and I are third to perform tonight. The fifteen-year-old girl currently on stage will be a tough act to follow. She sings like nobody's business. I have to wonder how it's possible for someone that age to have so much stage presence. The song isn't memorable, but her delivery is.

"Think she was singin' when she came out of her mama's womb?" Thomas asks me now.

I shake my head and smile a little. "Maybe. Is it me, or do the newbies get younger every day?"

We're both standing at the back of the room, me with my guitar, Thomas chewing gum like it's the fuel for every note he plans to reach when it's our turn to go on stage.

"They get younger every day," Thomas says.

The girl's guitar goes suddenly quiet, and she smacks out a beat below the strings, urging the crowd to follow along. They do while she does a stretch of a cappella that reveals even more fully the sweet tone of her voice.

Thomas starts to clap. "Kinda grows on you, doesn't she?"

"She's got what it takes to get her there."

"Yup."

If we've learned anything at all in the past year and a half of navigating Nashville's music industry waters, it is that talent is only a piece of it. Talent steps off the bus in this town every single day, and, with equal frequency, talent leaves. Making it here is about way more than just mere ability. "Think she'll see it through?" I ask.

"Depends on how many dents she gets in that guitar of hers and how quickly they come, I guess. Although I'd say it's gonna take some hefty whacks to derail that little girl's mojo."

I can't disagree with him. I've met some incredible singers in the past year and a half who seemed like they could take the knocks, most

1

having arrived in Nashville full of the confidence built by small-town accolades and family praise. But most people have a vulnerability of some kind, and the music business has a way of unearthing it, even when it's hidden way down deep.

The girl ends the song, and the crowd responds with enthusiastic applause. She all but glows with it, and I wonder if my time here has already rubbed some of that shine from my enthusiasm.

She introduces Thomas and me then, my stomach plummeting as it always does right before we perform.

"If you've been in Nashville any time at all," she says, "you've probably already heard about these two. Good heavens, can they sing! Ladies and gentlemen, give it up for Barefoot Outlook!"

"Let's do this thing," Thomas says, dropping his gum in a trash can and waving me ahead of him with a gentlemanly bow.

On stage, Thomas does the introductions, his Georgia drawl full tilt. "Hey everybody, I'm Thomas Franklin. This is CeCe MacKenzie. We're Barefoot Outlook, and we're pleased as pickle juice to be here with y'all tonight!"

If the girl before us has stage presence, Thomas is the polished version of it. Since we first started performing together, I've been in awe of the way he wins the interest and attention of the crowd in front of us before he ever sings a note.

"If y'all came to Nashville to hear some country music," he says, "then hold on, 'cause here we go."

Anyone who's never seen Thomas perform with Holden wouldn't realize that he's different when they're onstage together. But I do. The two of them had this rapport that translated into something I don't think Thomas and I will ever have. Maybe it comes from having been best friends for so long and knowing pretty much all there is to know about a person. Like two people who've been married for decades and can guess what the other will order in a restaurant before they even open the menu. And like two people who fell in love and got married when they were really young, Thomas and Holden will always be each other's first for writing music and performing. I have never been under any illusion that I am a replacement for Holden.

Holden. A year and a half since he's been gone, and he still skitters through my thoughts at random points throughout every single day. He writes songs and sends them to Thomas on a regular basis, but he hasn't returned to Nashville even once since the night he left to go back to Atlanta, back to Sarah.

Our first song tonight is "Country Boys Don't Wear Thongs." Holden sent it to Thomas a couple of weeks ago. It's upbeat, twangy, and funny and immediately sets the mood for our performance. Thomas sells it like bottled water in the Sahara Desert. By the end of the last chorus, the crowd is fully hooked. It's what we wait for when we're onstage, and it's like searching for the right key and knowing the sound when the lock clicks into place.

When Thomas and I first started playing together after Holden left Nashville, we were like two people on a blind date, unsure of what to say, both letting the other go first, the result being that a couple of our shows were pretty much a muddled mess.

The next is Holden's as well, a duet called "Our Back Fence." The third is "What You Took From Me," the song Holden wrote about a man who lost his wife to a drunk driving accident. And the last song we perform is one I wrote called "Don'tcha Do That." It brings the crowd back up, and at the end, Thomas thanks everyone for being here and lets them know we'll be playing tomorrow night at the Rowdy Howdy.

Just before we leave the stage, he throws out, "Y'all come on down and let us show you a good time!"

The clapping follows us to the back of the room where Thomas gets my guitar case and hands it to me. We chat while I put my guitar away and discuss a couple of moments during the first song we think we could have handled better.

"Hey, there's someone out here who wants to talk to you two."

I look up to see the fifteen-year-old who performed before us smiling at me with the kind of smile that makes it clear life has not yet dealt her a single hard blow.

"Who is it?" Thomas asks.

She shrugs. "Some guy in a suit. Want me to tell him to come on back?"

"Sure," Thomas says. "That's fine."

She turns to go and then swings around. "Hey, by the way, y'all were awesome up there. You write your own stuff?"

"CeCe wrote a couple of the songs. The rest were written by a friend of ours."

"Wow, they're really good," she says. "I hope I can write like that some day."

"Just keep at it," Thomas says.

"I will. See y'all soon." She waves once and is gone.

My phone vibrates. I glance at the text. It's Beck, letting me know he's running a little late to pick me up.

I text back. "NP. See you in a few."

"K" is his reply.

"Beck?" Thomas asks.

"Yeah."

"Where y'all headed tonight?"

"His dad's having a thing," I say.

"A thing at Case Phillips's house is a good thing, isn't it?"

"Yeah. I guess I'm tired."

"Of Beck?"

I look up quickly. "No. Why?"

"Just seems like you haven't been seeing him as much as you were."

"We've both been busy," I hedge.

"Okay."

"We have!" I insist.

"Okay," Thomas says with a smile. "Me thinks she doth protest too much."

"Stop," I say. "And anyway, you're the one who needs to get your love life out of drought status."

"Ouch! Low blow."

"You opened that can of worms."

A knock sounds against the frame of the doorway. A man in a dark suit steps in and says, "I was told I could find you two back here."

"Yes, sir," Thomas says. "What can we do for you?"

"I'm Andrew Seeger." He walks forward and sticks his hand out to me. We shake, and he pumps Thomas's hand as well. "I'm hoping I can do something for you."

During our first months in town, this would have perked our ears up considerably. Fancy guy, fancy suit, do something for us. It's certainly not the first time we've heard it. To date, not much of it has panned out.

"Yeah?" Thomas says. "What's that?"

Andrew doesn't appear put off by Thomas's shortness. "The song you did tonight. "What You Took From Me." Did one of you write it, or both of you?

Thomas shakes his head. "A buddy of ours wrote it."

"Oh." Andrew appears slightly disappointed. "Is he around?"

"Actually, no," Thomas says. "He lives in Atlanta now."

Andrew looks more disappointed.

"What exactly is this about?" Thomas asks.

"I'm Hart Holcomb's manager."

At the name, my eyes go wide, and I feel Thomas's surprise as well.

"A friend told us about the song," he says, his voice soft. "Hart snuck into a club downtown where you two were playing and listened for himself. Hart's wife was killed in a drunk driving accident five years ago. The message is one he feels a need to put out there, and well, he loved it. He wants to record it."

I glance at Thomas, see the look of stunned surprise on his face, and realize mine probably mirrors it exactly.

"Did you say Hart Holcomb?" Thomas asks.

"Yeah," Andrew says with a half-smile. "Hart had just finished up his new record when somebody told him about it. He's bumping another song to include this. I gotta tell you, if there's any such thing as a lucky break for a songwriter, this is it. Think you can get your friend down here, like ASAP?"

Under most circumstances, the answer would be an immediate yes, but Thomas had yet to talk Holden into coming back even once. After his last trip to Atlanta to see Holden, Thomas returned with the admission that maybe it was time he accepted that Holden was through. "He said he'd write songs for me as long as I want him to," he'd admitted, more down than I'd ever heard him, "but anything else, he's moved on."

"I'm not really sure," Thomas says now, and I flash a quick look at him.

Andrew hands Thomas a card. "My number is on there. Ask him to give me a call and let me know when we can meet with Hart."

"Will do," Thomas says.

"All right, then." Andrew drops us a nod and walks out.

Thomas and I look at each other but wait a full sixty seconds before saying a word.

"Did he just say Hart Holcomb wants to record Holden's song?" Thomas is smiling.

"Yeah, he did."

"Good friggin' day! That's like somebody dropping in to say you won the lottery when you didn't even buy a ticket."

"It's a great song," I say, deliberately keeping my voice smooth.

"It is."

"Do you think he'll come?"

Thomas's smile fades instantly. "He has to come. If I have to drive down there and drag his butt here myself, he's coming."

I don't doubt Thomas means it, but I also know that Holden has chosen another life and made it clear that this one is behind him. Something flutters low inside me at the thought of seeing him again. It shouldn't, but it does.

"In fact, I'm calling him right now." Thomas pulls his phone from his shirt pocket, swipes the screen and then taps his number.

My heart kicks into overdrive now. Which is ridiculous considering I'm not the one calling, and Holden won't even know I'm in the room. My palms instantly start to sweat. I pick up my guitar and mouth to Thomas, "I'm leaving. Beck is…"

"Hold on a minute," Thomas says. "Don't go anywhere."

Holden answers because Thomas says, "Hey, what are you doing?" A pause and, "You're still at work? I thought the corporate world went home at five." Another pause. "Are you sitting down? Well you should. We just finished up a set at the Blue Bird."

I notice he doesn't say my name.

"And you're not gonna believe what's happened. Hart Holcomb wants to record "What You Took From Me." Silence and then, "Ah, hold on, maybe you didn't understand what I said. *Hart Holcomb* wants to record your song. This is pretty much a once in a lifetime opportunity. Can you come down tomorrow, man?"

A pause before, "Seriously! Two years ago, you would have sold your eyeteeth for a chance like this. . .Yeah, I know things are different now, but do you have to stop living. . .Well, not the life you planned to live."

Another stretch of awkward silence. Thomas says, "You know what, I'm going to pretend for now that somebody hit you over the head with a two-by-four, and you're not yourself. I'll call back in the morning and hope the Holden I used to know will answer the telephone." And with that he clicks off.

It's a rare thing to see Thomas angry. I've seen him mildly aggravated a couple of times, but this is far beyond that.

"Aliens have taken over his body," he says, looking at me and shaking his head.

"He made a choice, Thomas."

"But he said she's doing well. It's like he thinks if he resumes his life, she'll get sick again."

"Maybe that's how he's made peace with it," I say, even though something at the core of me aches with a deep dull throb. I had made my own peace with it eventually; not right away, because it simply hurt too much. Watching Holden go and not come back was the first time in my life I fully understood the meaning of wanting something heart and soul and not being able to have it. Before that, if I had been asked, I would have said I knew what that felt like. There had been things in my life that I didn't get, that I yearned for at the time. I didn't get the puppy I wanted for Christmas when I was seven. I didn't make the cheerleading squad in tenth grade. And after standing in line for almost two days to audition for *American Idol*, I came down with the stomach flu and had to leave.

By world standards, those are ridiculously minuscule things, but in nineteen years of life, those events were my measuring stick for disappointment. Maybe it's their flimsiness that made wanting Holden and not being able to have him all the more excruciating.

On the morning he left, I lay in bed listening to the sounds of his going. The shower starting up in his room. The zip of his luggage. The snap of his guitar case. The squeak of the bedroom door. His footsteps in the hallway. The gush of water from the kitchen faucet. Muffled words between him and Thomas, their tones low and somber. Then the opening of the door and the clicking sound of it closing behind him. I had been holding the tears inside. With that final sound of his leaving, they had gushed up and out of me with the force of a geyser. It was as if my holding them in had only increased the pressure beneath, and I could not stop myself from sobbing. I buried my face in my pillow, but Thomas heard me and came into the room.

Sitting down on the side of the bed, he pulled me up against him. He folded his arms around me like a big, broad band of comfort, and he let me cry. I cried until there wasn't a single tear left in me. I lay limp and empty against his wide strong chest. He rubbed the back of my hair with one hand and said, "Damn, it sucks."

"I'm not just crying for me," I'd said. "I'm crying for all of it. How could someone so young, how could she-"

"I don't know," Thomas said, shaking his head. "It's a wretched fuck of a disease."

I bit my lower lip and refused to let another dry sob slip past my throat. "Will she be okay?" I asked, like a small child looking to a parent for reassurance of things simply too big to process.

He continued rubbing my hair. "I pray like hell she will."

"I didn't mean to fall in love with him," I said in little more than a whisper.

Thomas said nothing for a bit, and I wondered if he hadn't heard me. But then he said, "I don't think he meant to fall in love with you either."

And that, just that, broke the dam again. Thomas had held me and let me cry. At some point, he slipped us both under the covers, and he stayed there with me until sleep stole my tears and gave me relief. An unbreakable bond was forged between the two of us that night. Our loss was mutual. It would be a while before either of us knew the extent of it, knew that Holden wasn't coming back for good. Once that became clear, something in Thomas dimmed a little. Holden had not only been like a brother to him, but was probably the only other person in the world who understood what music meant to him and felt the same way about it. They had been on a journey together for a long time, and when Holden's path had veered off in another direction, Thomas was just kind of lost. Everything he thought he'd wanted to do in this town was now up for question.

He'd been in the living room one night when I got home from working in the restaurant. He was sitting on the couch with Hank Junior nestled up under the crook of his arm, his head on Thomas's lap. I know my Hank, and I could tell by the look on his face that he was worried about Thomas.

"Everything okay?" I asked, dropping my purse on the coffee table. Hank thumped his tail, looked up, and licked Thomas's cheek.

"I swear your dog has telepathy," Thomas said.

I walked over and rubbed Hank's head. "So what's wrong?"

"I've been thinking. Maybe I ought to hang up this gig too."

I felt my eyes go wide, my lips part in surprise. "You mean quit music? Leave Nashville?"

"Well, it's kinda not making much sense now. Without Holden, I'm not sure it will ever work for me."

I sat down on the sofa next to him. "I know you miss him," I said.

"I think maybe I never realized quite how much of the driving force he was behind the two of us. Heck, CeCe, I just like to sing. I'm not any good at writing or scheduling gigs. That was Holden's thing. And it all...well, it feels flat without him."

I wanted to disagree, but I couldn't. It was like going on vacation to a place normally completely sunny, only to have your seven days there filled with clouds and rain. Somehow, it wasn't the same. "Would he want you to leave, to give all this up?"

"Well, no, but that's not really the point. He doesn't get to say whether I do or not."

I studied him for a moment and then said, "I'm not sure you know exactly how much of a gift you have in that voice of yours. People love to hear you sing, Thomas, and you love to do it. I bet, if you asked him,

Holden would keep writing for you. He loves to write. I can't imagine that he would give that up forever."

"I think he wants to forget all of it."

"You don't know until you ask."

We sat there on the couch for a good long while. Now that I was home to take over soothing duty, Hank Jr. snored softly, his head still resting on Thomas's leg.

"Assuming that he does want to keep writing," Thomas said finally, "and that's a big 'does,' what about the two of us going on with the Barefoot Outlook thing? I know you've been doing your thing, and I've been doing mine but I don't much like being solo."

"Me, either," I said. And even though it wasn't what I had once imagined for myself, I realized that I did like what we had begun putting together as Barefoot Outlook. Before Sarah's diagnosis and Holden's leaving. "Think it will fly with just the two of us?" I asked.

"Won't know until we try."

Since that night, that's what we've been doing. Holden did agree to continue writing, and most of the songs he's sent us were written to include us both. All of our communication went through Thomas. And I hadn't spoken to him since the morning he left the apartment. I guess it's better that way because what would there have been for us to say to each other?

Holden did the right thing. I have not questioned this, even at its cost to me. From the moment Sarah's diagnosis became a reality, I never once thought that he would choose me. I never once thought that he would do anything but the right thing where Sarah was concerned.

A person can only be what they are, and what I know about Holden is this. He's the guy who's going to walk the little old lady across the street, pick up the starving dog on the side of the road. He's the guy who sees right as right, and wrong as wrong, and there's no in between, no gray. Because if he hadn't been that guy, it's as simple as this. I would never have fallen in love with him.

♪

Holden

It's nine-thirty by the time I leave the office and head home. I take Peachtree Road out of downtown Atlanta, choosing traffic over the interstate. The Volvo belongs to Sarah's father's company. As an employee there, part of my compensation package includes a vehicle to drive. I had actually put up an argument over being given such an expensive ride for an entry level position, but Dr. Saxon is not a man too many people win an argument against. My job is a good one, a job most college graduates would be thrilled to get just coming out of school. And under any other circumstances, having the opportunity to work with Dr. Saxon would feel like something of a coup.

Sarah's father is a smart guy. His first invention, over twenty years ago, made him a multimillionaire. He developed a cream for burn victims that accelerated the healing process by as much as thirty percent. From there, he created other medicinal products, mostly rooted in natural sources, that were eventually sold to pharmaceutical companies and put his worth at over two hundred million dollars.

In fact, it is probably Dr. Saxon's unyielding determination to help Sarah beat her disease that got her to where she is now, in remission, feeling and looking like herself again. I wonder sometimes what would have happened had he not pushed her from clinic to clinic, including one in Mexico, trying countless methods of boosting her body's immune system. Watching him do everything in his power to help her made me wonder many times if he was fighting not only for Sarah's life, but his own as well. I really believe that if Sarah had died, he would have too.

That kind of love isn't something I ever saw growing up in my own home. My father's love had never been rooted in selflessness. I'm sure there was a reason for it. Maybe it was my mother's leaving when I was six and the house suddenly becoming a place where Dad and I basically crossed paths and little more. He saw his role as raising me, preparing me for the world and then pushing me out into it.

I know that's what a parent is actually supposed to do, but my dad's efforts always felt as if they were rooted in obligation. As for Sarah's parents, especially her father, everything he did for her stemmed from the purest kind of love, a love I have often wondered if anyone else in her life will be able to live up to.

Our apartment is in a nice section of Buckhead, in between the Buckhead Diner and Phipps Plaza. It's actually a condominium that Dr. Saxon bought for Sarah about six months after she got her first clear checkup. It's in a high-rise, its only drawback being that Patsy absolutely hates the elevator and refuses to get in unless I'm carrying her. I've discovered that an older Beagle pretty much personifies stubbornness. When the two of us moved in here with Sarah, I expected Patsy to be a permanent bone of contention between us, but somewhere along the way, Sarah decided that my having a dog wasn't such a bad thing. Although she still doesn't like for her to sit on the couch or sleep on our bed, she's okay with her. I should say they're okay with each other.

I park in the garage and take the elevator to our floor. As soon as I stick the key in the lock, I hear Patsy click, click, clicking across the tile. She is waiting just inside the door, as she is every night when I get home.

Her tail a wagging blur, she's so happy to see me that she's shaking, and I wonder, not for the first time, why anyone would choose to be lonely. All they have to do is get a dog. No one has bothered to tell Patsy that I actually did not hang the sun and the moon, and so she continues to think I did. I have to admit I don't mind. I reach down and rub under her chin where she likes to be rubbed. "Do you need to go out? Have you been out already?"

She jogs in place like a little foot soldier, and I feel a surge of pride for how good she looks. Her coat is shiny, and although she's not plump, she looks like a dog who is well-fed and well-loved. In the Davidson County pound, she had looked at least twice as old as she does now. I guess it's true that while lack of care can age beyond fairness, it is also true that the simple ingredients of kindness and love can peel away those years.

"I took her out about a half hour ago."

I look up to see Sarah standing in the kitchen doorway, a soft smile on her mouth. She's thin in skinny jeans and a pink sweater; her hair still very short, but thick and again healthy.

"Thanks," I say. "I didn't mean to be this late."

"That's okay. We had a nice walk."

"Smells great in here."

"I'm roasting some vegetables," she says. "Hungry?"

"Starving."

"Get your shower, and I should have everything ready by the time you're done."

"Sounds good," I say. I walk over and give her a kiss on the cheek, patting my leg for Patsy to follow me. Instead, she leads the way, and in the bedroom, heads for the fancy dog bed Sarah bought for her when we moved in.

Fatigue hits me in a wave as I step under the shower spray a few minutes later. I lean against the wall and let it do its best to revive me. It's not as if my work is physical. It isn't. I've been doing research for Dr. Saxon on hundreds of different topics, compiling the most relevant notes for whatever question he has presented me with. It's interesting, so I'm not exactly sure why I come home exhausted each night.

But then a thought waves itself in front of me like a white flag vying to be noticed. Round pegs, square hole. The constant forcing of a fit. Trying to make something function in a manner in which it was not designed to function. I try not to think about it, belabor it, question it.

I made a choice. Just over nineteen months ago, I made a choice. It's not one I can regret, or really ever imagine regretting.

The first weeks after I came back to Atlanta were a complete nightmare, for Sarah, for me, for her family. The diagnosis itself, the suggested forms of treatment. Chemo. Complete mastectomy with reconstruction. The prognosis itself, unwavering in its uncertainty. It wasn't an if-then proposition. If you take this treatment, then you will be cured. With her cancer, there was nothing definite except for the fact that it had taken her body hostage.

The gratitude on Sarah's face that first night back in Atlanta told me, as nothing else could, that I'd made the right choice. None of what had happened between us in Nashville mattered at that point. She never brought it up, and I never mentioned it. We went on as before, like I had never left Atlanta to go there in the first place. Like there had never been CeCe.

Her name is like a small electrical shock to my brain, because I don't let myself think it very often. There's no point in dwelling on something that can no longer be. It's not as if I were able to do it in the beginning, put her out of my mind. I think I know now that the heart doesn't give up what it wants that easily. I have no explanation for how hard I fell or how fast except that it was like finding a part of myself that I never realized was missing until I met her.

Thomas's call is suddenly front and center, and that's another thing there's no point in thinking about. I'm not going back to Nashville. The likelihood of Hart Holcomb actually cutting my song is about as probable as Georgia snow in July. To go back on the off chance that something might come of it doesn't seem worth what it would feel like to have to leave again. Easier not to go back at all.

I put on sweat pants and a t-shirt and head for the kitchen. Sarah has dinner on the table. We sit down with her telling me about a nutrition class she is taking. In addition to the juicing she's been doing, she's considering adapting to a completely raw diet.

"With the way you like salads," I say, "that shouldn't be too hard."

"I think so too," she agrees. "Some of the research the professor presented was pretty convincing."

"Then you definitely should."

She spears a red pepper, looks at me for a moment and then says, "Are you okay?"

"Yeah," I say.

"You look, I don't know, a little sad or something."

"I'm just tired."

"Daddy over-working you?"

I shake my head. "I probably didn't sleep great last night."

"Anything bothering you?"

"No. Everything's good." I'd like to think I sound convincing but she doesn't look convinced.

A couple of hours later when we're in bed, Sarah reaches across and clasps her fingers in mine. Her touch surprises me. For a long time after her surgery, she did not want me to touch her. Even after her body had completely healed physically, she avoided any opportunity for us to be close.

I've let myself think that with time, this part of our relationship would come back. So far it hasn't. We've continued to ignore it, even though it's begun to loom between us like a big black cloud that we can no longer see through. With her fingers entwined in mine, she says, "Thomas called earlier, right before you got home."

Something jumps inside my chest, and I realize there's no point in asking her what he wanted. "Did he?"

"He told me about the song," she says.

"Yeah, you know the odds of that becoming anything."

She's quiet for a minute or more before saying, "Maybe it's time we talk about some of that."

"What is there to talk about?" I ask, deliberately nonchalant. "Another time, another place."

"But it was your dream."

"Was," I say.

She sighs, turns over onto her side, and, with a fingertip under my jaw, forces me to look at her. "Dreams don't really go away, do they?"

"Sometimes they have to," I answer, my tone ragged enough that I immediately wish I had censored it.

She's quiet for several moments before saying, "Can we drop the walls and be honest with one another, Holden?"

"Sarah," I look at the ceiling, "I am being honest with you."

"I know you think you are. Holden, before I knew I was sick, what I wanted more than anything was for you to come back here because it was where you wanted to be. I never pretended that Nashville was my dream, and I guess I wanted you to decide that it wasn't yours either. But it was your dream. Still is your dream."

"You know I've put all that behind me," I say.

"I know you think you have." She squeezes my hand hard, as if bracing herself. "I want you to go back."

"What?" I hear the surprise in my voice.

"If you don't, you'll regret it," she says softly, "because you'll always wonder what might have happened."

"No, I won't," I say, firm.

Sarah turns over on her back and now she is staring at the ceiling as well. Patsy snores softly, one *z* after another, all that is filling the silence between us.

"Sarah, things are good now. Let's not mess it up, okay?"

"But are they? Really good? Compared to what they could have been, yes, I think they are. Good as in, I didn't die."

I sit up on one elbow. "Don't talk like that."

"I could have, it's true."

"You didn't, and you won't."

"At least not if Daddy has anything to say about it," she says, a half-smile on her mouth. "I don't know, Holden, I guess I've been thinking a lot about how I'm different now."

"What do you mean?"

"How we're all just one doctor's visit and diagnosis away from our lives being shattered as we know them. I know now how in a blink it can all change. I was so arrogant about life and what I thought I deserved."

"You weren't arrogant," I say.

"Actually, I was. I wanted you, at whatever cost, even if it meant that you would never really be happy with the life that we made together."

"Sarah," I take her hand again, "I am happy. Stop."

"You made a choice to give up all the things that you wanted. You made a choice to give up your writing and music, and I let you because I was too selfish to let you go."

"That's not true."

"It is true," she insists. "And if I couldn't let you go and be sure that you would come back, were you ever really mine to begin with?"

I'd like to answer, to reassure her with the words I know she needs to hear, but they're stuck somewhere in the back of my throat and for the life of me I cannot force them out.

"Now that I'm admitting all of this, I guess I want to be loved by someone else the way I've loved you, Holden. I don't think I want to go through the rest of my life being the one who loves the most."

"Sarah, please-"

"Let me finish. We both deserve that."

"Why are you doing this?" I ask, feeling as if I'm walking on glass and everything beneath me is going to shatter at any second.

"Because I know you won't ever do it first."

Her words fall around us like rain pinging off a roof. I try to absorb their meaning. "Are you saying everything that's happened in this past year and a half has meant nothing?"

"No," she says softly. "The opposite. It's meant everything. What you did for me when you knew that I needed you. . .I don't have any words to come close to thanking you for being who you are. But there is something I can do to pay you back."

"What?" I ask, not sure I even want to know the answer.

"Let you go. Without guilt or regret."

"Sarah-"

"Go and be who you were meant to be, Holden."

"I don't know why you're saying these things. This is a mistake."

"It isn't. And I don't want to think of any of it that way. But to hold onto each other for the wrong reasons, yes. That would be a mistake."

I slip an arm around her waist and pull her to me, a deep sadness sinking in around me. Because she's right. I know she's right.

She presses her face into my chest, and I feel her tears against my skin. "We don't have to do this," I say.

She puts a finger to my lips. "There is one more thing."

Hearing something different in her voice, I pull back to look at her. "What?"

She's silent until I start to think she's not going to tell me. "I've met someone, Holden."

The words hang in the space between us, and I see in her expression that she's not sure what my reaction will be. "A guy?" I ask, the question sounding flat and disbelieving even to my ears.

She nods once, biting her lower lip.

"Who?" I ask, and I don't think my voice sounds like my own.

She hesitates and then, "He's one of the doctors I've been seeing for my follow-up care. Nothing has happened. But he's told me he has feelings for me. And I. . .I think I might for him, too."

I sit up, swing my legs over the side of the bed, lean forward with my elbows on my knees and pull in a couple of deep breaths. "That is probably the last thing in the world I expected to hear you say."

"I didn't go looking for it. And if things were truly right between us, I don't think it would have found me."

When I can speak, I say, "Is all of this because of the very unlikely possibility of me getting a cut on my song?"

"No," she says, placing a hand on my back in what feels like a gesture of comfort. "It's just the trigger."

♪

CeCe

It's one a.m., and the party at Beck's dad's place looks like it's just getting started. There are enough famous faces in various parts of this house to keep a paparazzi photographer snapping away in every direction. The pool is shaped like a guitar, and two of the guys in Case's band are sitting on the diving board, taking requests, one song after another.

I'm in a chair at the opposite end when Beck returns from getting us both a drink. "Here you go," he says, handing me my glass of San Pellegrino and lime.

"Thanks." I look up at him with what I can feel is a weak attempt at a smile.

He sits down on the chair beside me, hip bumping me over a bit. "Hey. What's wrong?"

"Nothing." I shrug and take a sip of the fizzy water.

"Beg to differ. You haven't been yourself all night. Show at the Blue Bird not go well?"

"It went great," I say, a little too bright even to my own ears. "Everything's good."

He puts a finger beneath my chin and forces me to look at him. "Give me credit for knowing you better than that."

"I guess I'm tired. It's been kind of a long week."

"You're working a lot. Why don't you cut back on your hours at the restaurant?"

"And eat with what?" I ask with a half-smile.

"You know I want to help you out, babe. You won't let me."

"I'm good, Beck. Seriously," I say, immediately digging in my heels as I do every time he brings this up.

"Just too tired to play," he says, and for a moment, it feels like I am way older than he is.

"Responsibility calls." I immediately regret my sharpness.

Beck leans back and gives me a long look. "Whoa. Where did that come from?"

"I'm sorry," I say instantly, feeling further guilt for something I'm not even sure I can identify. Beck and I have been officially seeing each other for almost a year now, and I've never once picked a fight. We've never actually *had* a fight.

"Sorry for what?" he asks, the question sounding a little bruised.

"For being a jerk."

"You're not a jerk," he says, putting an arm around my shoulders and pulling me to him. He presses a kiss to my cheek and then nips my lower lip before kissing me full and deep. I respond as I know I should. Kissing him back and telling myself as I have a dozen times before that I would be an idiot to throw this away.

Beck Phillips is all but an actual commodity in Nashville. The only son of a major country music star. Good-looking beyond fairness. How many times have I waited for him at the end of one of his classes at Vanderbilt and seen the girls following him around like puppies after a treat jar? And every time, I've asked myself, why me? Of all the girls he could have in this town, why me?

If I've found anything close to an answer, I would say it's this. Beck doesn't like losing. He likes winning. Not in an obnoxious, arrogant sort of way. It's just what he's used to. Having what he wants. Whether it's right away. Or eventually. And maybe that's what fueled his interest in me. I've yet to give him all of me. Emotionally or physically.

He kisses my neck now, one hand looped around my waist. "Let's go up to my room," he says. "You can take a nap."

I smile and repeat one of my granny's favorite sayings. "Do I look like I just fell off the turnip truck?"

He laughs. "No, I don't guess you do," he says, kissing me full on again. He studies me without bothering to hide the need in his eyes. "What if I promise to be good?"

"I need to go home and sleep in my own bed."

"We could do that."

This time, I laugh. "No one ever said you're not persistent."

He loops an arm around my waist and lifts me onto his lap, kissing me deeply. When he pulls back, he says, "Desperation breeds persistence."

"All right, lovebirds, this is a public gathering." Case Phillips ruffles Beck's hair, saving me from a response.

"Dad," Beck protests, swatting his hand away. It's really a weird thing, knowing who Case Phillips the country music star is most of my life and then to see Beck act as if he is any regular dad who irritates him the way most dads irritate their teenage sons.

Case reaches for a chair and pulls it up next to ours. He's holding a beer in one hand, but it's nearly full. I've noticed he doesn't drink as much as the people he surrounds himself with. He sits and leans back with his long legs stretched out in front of him.

"Dad," Beck repeats, "we're kind of busy."

"I can see you're working hard in that direction," Case agrees with a raised eyebrow.

I feel the blush start in my cheeks and level out at my hairline. I slide off Beck's lap and sit beside him on the lounge chair.

"I didn't come over to ruin the party," Case says, an apology in his voice. "I actually have a proposition for you both."

"What?" Beck struggles to dampen his aggravation.

"My opening act for the upcoming tour seems to be falling apart before everybody's eyes."

"Footfalls?" Beck asks.

Case nods.

"Why?" Beck sounds more interested now. "They're crazy good."

"Agreed. Which is why a person has to wonder why they want to throw all that away by showing up for rehearsals late and loaded."

"Drugs?" Beck says, looking surprised.

"Who the hell knows? I would assume. But you know I don't stand for that crap on tour. They've been given three warnings, and it hasn't made a difference yet. Paula didn't make it through the first set this afternoon."

"I know Paula," I say, unable to hide my surprise. "We've written a couple of songs together. I can't believe she would–"

"No one ever does," Case says. "Who can figure the human psyche? Sometimes getting what you want comes with more pressure than some people can handle."

I get that, but I've had several long conversations with Paula about our love for music and the hope that we'll get to do this our whole lives. She's a small-town girl from South Carolina who has the support of a family who've given their all to help her get where she is. We were writing together the day she got the news that her band had been chosen to tour with Case. I nearly had to peel her off the wall. How could she willingly throw it all away? "That really doesn't seem like something she would do. Does she know they're at risk of being asked to leave the tour?"

"I'm afraid we're already past the at-risk phase. They're gone. Out of my hands."

"That sucks," Beck says.

"Yeah. It does suck to see someone throw away something they've worked so hard for."

My heart actually hurts for Paula and everything I know she has just lost.

"I had a thought this afternoon," Case says. "Rhys played that demo we did in the studio, what a year, year and a half ago, with you and your friends, CeCe?"

I nod. "Yes, sir."

He raises an eyebrow at me. "Wish you'd quit with the sir stuff, hon. You make me feel like a founding member of Mount Rushmore."

I smile. "Sorry, Case. You're not, you know."

His grin says he's totally aware that he's still got it as far as most American females are concerned. "I know Holden and Sarah moved back to Atlanta, but you and Thomas have a great thing going. What would you think about Beck joining the group and y'all stepping in as my opening act?"

I hear him say the words, but they don't completely sink in. I feel sure I must have imagined them. "What? Are you serious?"

"Dead," he says.

Adrenaline rushes up from the pit of my stomach, and I wish Thomas were here to take this in at the same time I am. I glance at Beck and notice his surprise. Case has pretty much done his best to keep Beck in school and out of the music business.

"Why now, Dad?" he asks, disbelief at the edge of the question.

Case sighs and shoves a hand through his dark hair. "Let's just say that after this last set of grades, it's becoming clear to me that you don't want to be in school any more than I did at your age. I know I've forced the issue. Maybe if you get out there and see what it's like, you'll want to go back at some point."

Beck raises his palm and high-fives his dad. "Heck, yeah!" he says. He looks at me then, as if he's forgotten that I have yet to say anything about his joining Thomas and me. "CeCe? What do you think?"

"I think it's an amazing opportunity," I say carefully. "Thank you, Case. I'd like to say yes this very minute, but do you mind if I talk with Thomas first?"

"Of course, that's how any good team operates," Case says, standing. "Need to know something by ten tomorrow though. Sorry for the short notice. We're running on a tight schedule now. Sound good?"

I nod. "Case, thank you again so much. I really don't know what to say."

"Say you'll do it," he says with his trademark smile. "That's thanks enough."

He leaves then, heading for a group of people chatting on the other side of the pool.

Beck leans back and looks at me with narrowed eyes. "Am I missing something, or am I the only one who thinks what just happened is incredible?"

"It is incredible," I say.

"Then why the reserve?"

"I didn't feel like I could really speak for Thomas and me both."

"I get that. Are you sure it isn't more about the fact that he wants me included?"

The question catches me off guard. "No. Why would you think that?"

"I guess it's just the vibe I'm getting."

"Beck, don't look for something that's not there."

"I'm not looking. But it's definitely there."

I want to deny it, but the butterflies in my stomach are telling me I do have some concerns. "I don't know. Maybe I'm wondering how we go from never having played together other than the demo at your dad's studio to performing in front of sold-out crowds three weeks from now."

"We'll just work our tails off until then."

"What about finishing up the semester at school? How will you manage that?"

Beck glances away and leans forward with his elbows on his knees. "Yeah. That. I think Dad is playing one step ahead of the curveball."

"What do you mean?"

He blows out a sigh and looks like he doesn't want to say what he's going to say. "My grades this semester aren't going to cut it."

"Oh," I say, more than a little surprised. "I'm sorry."

"Now you think I'm a loser, right?" he says, his voice low and unsure.

"Of course not."

"The only reason I went there in the first place is because Dad wanted me to. I guess this is his way of throwing me a lifeline."

"Pretty nice lifeline," I say, trying for a smile.

He studies me for a moment, and then says, "You don't think it's fair, do you?"

"What?"

"Being handed this."

"Of course it's fair. He's your dad. That should count for something."

"You mean that?"

"I do."

"A lot of people think I have a silver spoon up my butt."

This makes me laugh. "Well, if they do, they don't know you."

"Thanks."

"Not necessary."

His expression goes suddenly serious. "I care what you think about me, CeCe."

There's a different note in the admission, one I haven't heard before. Vulnerability. And I'm not sure I know what to do with that.

♪

BECK TAKES ME home, and we say almost nothing during the drive back into town. With the BMW's top down, the wind provides a good excuse for silence although the space between us feels thick with Beck's unusual somberness.

I don't even know why I'm acting this way, why my response to this completely out-of-left-field opportunity isn't more of what it should be. As I stare out into the night whipping past us, I realize that my thoughts have been occupied with Holden on some level since Hart Holcomb's manager came back to see us after the show at the Blue Bird. I'd like to deny it, but then I wouldn't even be honest with myself.

When we arrive at the apartment, Beck doesn't turn off the car and get out to walk me up as he usually does.

"Let me know what you and Thomas decide," he says.

I can hear that his irritation has now melted into something much more like hurt. My guilt is instant. I reach across to cover his hand with mine. "I'm sorry, Beck, for being so difficult tonight."

"Hey, it is what it is."

"But it's not. Exactly."

He leans back against the seat and pulls his hand out from under mine. "Then what is it, CeCe? No, on second thought, don't answer that. Maybe what's happened tonight will serve a couple different purposes."

"What do you mean?"

"Force your hand, I guess. Look, I think we both know I'm the one who's been pushing you along in this relationship. Maybe I didn't want to admit that exactly, but I don't think I can deny it any longer. So while you're making up your mind about whether you want this gig with my dad, why don't you figure out whether you want me or not as well? And it's not an either or proposition. I want *you* and the gig. But if I can't have both-"

I lean over and kiss him, quick and full. I feel his resistance for several long seconds, but then he gives and pulls me to him. I blank my mind of everything except him and the fact that he has been there for me during this past year. He's made me part of his life, introduced me to everyone he knows in this town. And he has been. . .even as I'm kissing him, I'm searching for the exact description. Then it hits me like a splash of ice cold water: a distraction.

I sit back in my seat just as the last two words slam through me. From Holden.

I press my hand to my lips. They tingle from the intensity of Beck's kiss.

For the first time in a year and a half, anger blooms inside me. The petals unfold like the pink blooms on Mama's Rose of Sharon tree in our backyard when spring prods it from its winter hibernation. I've imagined many times how those blooms must resist that awakening, especially when warm weather is teasing its way into existence, and there's no guarantee that nighttime won't drape them with frost.

I think maybe I'm the Rose of Sharon in this situation, refusing to open my heart fully to Beck because somewhere inside of me, I am frozen with love for Holden. And I realize then that I'm angry with myself for that. Who stays in a holding pattern for this long? Waiting for something that's already passed? That can never come back? Never be what it might have been. I know now that as surely as I'm sitting here, that's what I've been doing. Waiting.

I don't want to wait any longer. Everything I've been working for, everything Thomas has been working for, is now right in front of us. Within reach. Only a fool would turn away from it.

"I want this, Beck," I say, linking my fingers through his. "I want you."

He's looking at me as if he's sure I didn't say what I just said. "What?"

"Don't act so surprised. You know you're hot." This brings a smile to his lips, and I think I may have redeemed myself, at least a little bit anyway. He leans across and kisses me again, and there's sweetness at the edges. Beck is a cool guy, and it's not in his playbook to show insecurity. I feel that now and the responsibility of it. An immediate desire not to take advantage of it.

"You won't regret it," he says softly. "Any of it. I promise, okay?"

"I know I won't," I say. "I'll talk to Thomas and call you." I glance at the clock. "It's already after three. In a few hours."

"Okay. Goodnight, CeCe."

"Night, Beck."

And with the closing of the car door, I feel something close inside me as well. If it's not gladness that follows the click, maybe acceptance is enough.

♪

HANK JUNIOR IS asleep on the couch when I unlock the door and step inside the apartment. He raises his head and blinks sleepy hound eyes at me then thumps his tail in greeting against the sofa cushion.

"Hey, sweet boy," I say, going over to sit down beside him. I rub his soft head and velvety ears. "Need to go out?"

He rests his chin on my leg and closes his eyes in answer. I try to talk myself into leaving the conversation with Thomas until morning, but the thought of sleeping with all of this on my mind is an absolute impossibility. I knock on his door and call out, "Thomas?"

A couple of seconds pass before he answers with a groggy, "That you, CeCe?"

"Yeah. Are you alone?"

"Actually, no, I'm not."

"Oh," I say, not doing a very good job of hiding my disappointment.

"Everything all right?" he calls out.

"I was hoping we could talk for a minute."

A pause and then, "You are aware that it's three o'clock in the morning?"

"Ah, yeah."

"And this is important?" he asks, as close to grouchy as he gets.

"It is," I say.

"I'll be out in a sec."

I wait for him in the hallway, and when he steps through the door, I try to peer over his shoulder. "Who is it?" I ask.

"None of your business," he says, turning me around and pushing me toward the living room with his hands on my shoulders.

"If it's a secret, she must not be very–"

He stops me with, "CeCe, what the devil are you getting me up at this hour for? Just to give me a hard time about who's in my bed?"

"I'm not," I say. "I mean, that's not why I got you up."

Thomas plops down on the couch beside Hank Junior. I take the chair across from them. He's wearing light blue boxers with banjos on them. I squint at them and say, "Nice."

"Do you really need me to go back and put on some britches?"

"No. I'll keep my eyes chest level or above."

"Thank you. Much appreciated," he says. "Are you planning on telling me why you got me up in the middle of the night?"

"Footfalls got fired as the opening act for Case's tour. He wants us to go in their place."

If I had just dropped, "Elvis is alive and coming over for dinner," I don't think Thomas could've looked any more surprised.

"Did you say-" he starts.

"I did," I interrupt.

A grin breaks his formerly sleepy expression wide open. "For real?"

"For real."

Several moments pass, during which he looks as if he has no idea where to go from here. And then, "What's the catch?"

"We have to be ready to perform as an opening act within three weeks."

He tips his head, considers this. "We're missing electric guitar, but we ought to be able to get that filled as soon as we put it out there as part of a tour opportunity."

"Yeah," I say.

"What else?"

"What do you mean?"

"What other catch? There must be one."

I hesitate before saying, "He wants Beck to join us." This one, I can see, he did not expect.

"Ah," he says. "So what's behind that?"

"Honestly?"

"Well, yeah."

"Beck has pretty much let his grades slide this semester. His dad has always discouraged him from getting into the music business but I guess he's realizing it's kind of inevitable."

"Dude can play guitar. No doubt about it."

"Think it could work?" I ask cautiously.

Thomas rubs Hank Junior's ears, quiet for a full minute or more. "I expect it's like this. If you and I have a brain in our heads, we'll find a way to make it work."

♪

Holden

My flight lands in Nashville at five-thirty-eight p.m. As the wheels touch the runway, my heartbeat kicks up a notch, and doubt pummels through me.

Yesterday at this time I hadn't even left work. I sure didn't know that in twenty-four hours, I would have turned my life upside down again, reaching out for a rope to grab onto that might or might not be there.

As I'd done a dozen times in the past several hours, I ask myself if I'm wrong to try to pick up the edges of a dream and roll it back into something recognizable. When I woke up this morning, my first thought was that Sarah would have changed her mind. That our conversation last night would reveal itself to be nothing more than a mistake in judgment.

I think that's what I was hoping because letting go of something I wanted so badly and coming to terms with that loss hadn't happened over night. And even if our lives hadn't turned out to be everything we had once imagined they could be, I did feel extreme gratitude for Sarah's recovery and the part she had told me I played in it.

She had not decided that it was a mistake in judgment. I'm not even sure the Sarah who helped me pack my things was the same Sarah I've known since college. I don't know exactly when it happened, but I could see in her face that she'd already moved on. Wanted something other than me now.

Maybe the only reason it doesn't hurt more is that I know she's right to want something else, some one else who will love her with every speck of space in his heart.

The way I wanted to. The way I tried to. It's pretty clear now that if I hadn't realized CeCe still occupied a corner of my heart, Sarah had.

A bell chimes, and the stewardess welcomes us to Nashville. Seat belts click their release in unison, and everyone around me stands up, reaching for bags and laptops. I start to stand, but something inside me locks my legs beneath a sudden rush of uncertainty.

It feels a lot like the time Thomas and I went skydiving our freshman year in college. He went first, and I remember standing at the edge of the plane door, watching him torpedo toward the ground. I could not make myself move. It was as if my brain and my legs were no longer synchronized. And as much as I hated the thought of disappointing him, I couldn't jump.

But then he looked up, waved a hand at me, and his parachute burst open, turning his descent into a graceful sashay through wide-open space.

That was the moment I stepped over the threshold of the plane and began the free fall. As soon as I was out there, dropping through the sky, I knew I wanted to do this a thousand more times. The only thing I've ever found to compare it to is music, every phase of it, from the creation of a first note in a new song to playing it on stage in front of an audience for the first time.

If starting out after this dream again is anything like skydiving, I know I'm going to have to take a leap of faith and jump. And so I stand up and join the exodus.

♪

THERE'S A DRIVER waiting at baggage claim with a sign that has my name on it. I walk over and tell him who I am.

"Well, all right," he says with the friendliness I remember as such a part of Nashville. "I'm Mitchell. Mr. Hart is expecting you, Mr. Ashford. Can I get your bag for you?"

"It's Holden, and thanks but I'm good." I follow him out the main doors and to a waiting Hummer limo. This, I hadn't expected.

He opens the back, takes my guitar and suitcase and puts them inside, then walks around to open the door for me.

"I can ride up front," I say, feeling about a dozen different kinds of awkward.

Mitchell smiles and shakes his head. "Hey, enjoy it, young man. Clearly, you've done something Mr. Hart appreciates. No need to feel guilty. Hop on in."

I slide inside and he closes the door behind me. The interior of the Hummer is a virtual entertainment playground; big screen TV and a music system that makes what's coming through the Bose speakers hanging in four corners sound like I'm at the Ryman Auditorium.

The limo glides away from the airport and onto the interstate. Through the tinted glass, I recognize the landscape and for the first time since this morning, I let myself feel happy about the thought of being here. I do, however, feel alone. That part doesn't seem right. I started this whole journey with my best friend in the world. And I realize I don't want to have this meeting with Hart Holcomb without him.

I reach forward and press an intercom button. "Mitchell?"

"Yes, Mr. Ashford?"

"Would it be possible for you to pick up a friend of mine on the way? I'd really like for him to come with me if you don't mind stopping."

"Of course. Do you have the address?"

I give it to him and sit back in my seat, texting Thomas: Hey. Where are you?

A few seconds pass before my phone beeps.

Home. Where are you?
Nashville.
Are you kidding me?
Would I?
Yes.
Get your boots on. I'm picking you up in   less than ten.
In what?
A stretch Hummer.
Dang.
Yeah.

He's waiting outside the building when we pull into the parking lot. It feels like we haven't seen each other in years, and I realize how much I've missed him. I open the door and slide out.

"You really are here," Thomas says, his grin full wattage, throwing me a high-five. "Aw, hell, brother. This deserves a hug."

He gives me exactly that, squeezing me so hard, I laugh and say, "Your neighbors are gonna get the wrong idea."

He lets me go, shaking his head, uncharacteristically at a loss for a response. "I can't believe you're really here. And in this ride?"

"Crazy, huh? Hart Holcomb sent it to pick me up at the airport."

"So you're meeting with him?"

I nod.

"Whoop!" Thomas yells. "Let's get on over there."

We climb in the back of the Hummer and Mitchell eases out of the parking lot.

Thomas can't quit grinning. "So this is what it's like when you make the big league," he says.

"I guess."

"He wants your song bad."

"I'm not assuming anything," I say.

"Would he go to all this trouble if he didn't?"

I shrug and say, "You haven't gotten any better-looking."

"And you're not any less of a smartass."

"True."

"Man, it's good to have you back. How long can you stay?"

I don't know how to begin explaining what's happened in the past day so I just start in the middle. "I guess until nobody wants to hear my music anymore."

Thomas tips his head, looking confused. "You mean you're here to stay? Like for good?"

I tell him then about Sarah and everything she'd said last night. And how I hadn't expected any of it. My voice is flat and without emotion, as if I am telling someone else's story instead of my own. When I finish, we both sit quiet for a minute or more.

"Is she okay?" Thomas asks, sounding a little shocked.

"She's better than okay. I don't know. I think it was a relief to her. To get it all said."

"Is it to you?" he asks, and I can tell he's not sure where to go with any of it either.

"It's the right thing for her," I say.

"And what about you?"

"I would have stayed."

"I know. Is your heart in one piece?"

"I think so. It's weird. I pretty much accepted that this life here was something I'd put behind me. I don't even really know how to start making music a focal point again."

"You don't think about it. You just do it. Start living it. You deserve it." He looks out the window and then back at me with a serious expression. "What you did for Sarah. I know what it cost you. In my book, they don't come any better than you, friend."

"Are you counting the part where I let myself fall in love with someone else while I was still officially with Sarah?"

"Yeah," he says, his voice firm. "I'm counting that part."

I tap a thumb against my jeans and try not to ask the question, but lose the battle. "How is she?"

"Good," Thomas says. "We've been playing somewhere about every night of the week. She's been working the lunch shift over at Lauren's."

"That's good."

"I take it you two haven't talked."

I shake my head.

"She's seeing Beck."

I'm not surprised. I expected it, really. Why wouldn't she, after all? "You like him?" I ask.

"Not much to dislike about him. But I'm pretty sure as far as she's concerned, he's not you."

"Hey, don't." I hold up a hand. "I'm not coming back here expecting anything between CeCe and me to change. If he's a good guy, good to her, that's all that matters."

"Is it?"

"Yeah," I say, wondering if I could sound any less convincing.

"If you say so."

The Hummer has left the interstate and is heading down a series of country roads that feature huge estate after huge estate. I remember that Case Phillips lives down one of the white-fenced lanes and wonder how much time CeCe has spent there with Beck, but then I cut the thought off as a dead end. There is nothing to be gained from going there.

Thomas and I make small talk the rest of the way. He tells me about the gigs they've been playing recently, and when I ask him if he's seeing anyone, he says no one special.

"Mr. Ashford?"

It's Mitchell on the intercom.

"Mr. Ashford," Thomas stage whispers, grinning at me.

"Yes?"

"We'll be arriving within a couple of minutes. Mr. Holcomb asked me to drop you at the horse barn if that's all right. He likes to ride in the evenings."

"Ah, sure. That's fine."

"Mr. Ashford at the horse barn," Thomas rap-teases.

"Shut up."

"Up yours."

"Nice to be back," I say.

"Nice to have you back," Thomas says.

♪

WE PULL INTO the cobblestone courtyard of a barn that looks more like a five-star English hotel than anything horses might live in. Boxwood bushes line each side of wrought iron-hinged sliding doors at the front. The exterior of the barn is stucco, the roof red clay tile. From either side of the entrance, horses peer over Dutch stall doors. One whinnies in our direction as we get out of the Hummer.

Mitchell walks around and says, "I'll be right out here when you're finished to give you a ride back into town."

"Thank you," I say.

At the sound of footsteps on the cobblestone, we glance up to see Hart Holcomb walking toward us. He's wearing a Stetson, Wranglers, and work boots. His shirt is wet in places, as if he's been sweating. He pulls it away from his midsection. "Sorry about the appearance. Working on some fencing out back."

"Not a problem," I say, stepping forward and sticking out my hand. "I'm Holden Ashford. This is my friend, Thomas Franklin. It's an honor to meet you, Mr. Holcomb."

"Hart, please. And thank you. For coming too." He shakes Thomas's hand as well and beckons for us to follow him into the barn.

The center aisle is also laid in cobblestone and it's so clean I'm pretty sure you'd be okay to eat off it. The interior stall doors are black with gold hinges, and they gleam with care and polish. Flies have been frequent visitors to the barns I've visited before, but I don't see one. Or even a single cobweb.

"What kind of horses do you have?" I ask, doing a quick estimate of stalls on either side of the aisle and coming up with a total of twenty-four.

"Quarter horses," he says. "We do a little cutting. Just for fun, mind you. My wife was a vegetarian, so anything that breathes on this farm isn't here to get eaten, cows included."

I hear something painful at the edges of his voice, and I'm not sure what to say to that. "She must have been a kind woman."

"She was."

"I'm really sorry for your loss."

Thomas murmurs his agreement.

"Thank you," Hart says. He stops in front of a stall to rub one of the horse's necks. "This was her baby. Whip is short for Whippoorwill. I think this horse might miss her as much as I do."

All three of us are silent for several moments before he goes on.

"It's a damn shame for the world to lose someone as fine as she was. And for no reason. When I heard your song, I felt like you might have written it for me," he says, his voice thickening with emotion.

"I can't think of a higher compliment than that," I say, and I realize how lame it sounds in comparison to this man's life-altering loss.

"I'd like for it to be the title song on my upcoming CD. You okay with that?"

I'm not sure what I had expected him to say when I got here, but it was anything other than this. I can't seem to find the words to answer him, so I simply nod.

"We'll need to go in the studio tomorrow. I've already thrown everything off schedule by adding this last minute. We'll be at HGT Recording downtown at ten. You boys want to come in for the session?"

"Yes, sir," Thomas and I answer in unison.

"Well, good deal," he says.

We shake hands. I like that his is firm, confirming.

"See you in the morning then. Mitchell will take you back into town."

He walks us to the barn entrance.

"Thank you, Mr. Holcomb, I mean Hart," I say. "This is such an honor."

"For me, too, actually," he says. "It's a hell of a song."

We climb in the back of the Hummer, and Mitchell eases out of the courtyard and down the long lane leading to the main road. Only then do I realize we never talked about money. And I don't care. If I could pay him to sing it, I would.

♪

CeCe

I'm coming up the stairs to our apartment, three Whole Foods bags in each hand when I hear their laughter.

There's no mistaking it. Thomas's big baritone. And Holden's slightly cautious follow-up.

My stomach plummets exactly the way it had on an awful elevator thrill ride I once went on at an amusement park. I can't recall how many stories it dropped. I remember it felt as if there were no bottom and we would never stop but just keep falling forever.

I pause on the top step now with that same sensation, making me light-headed, fight or flight battling it out inside me.

What is he doing here? In our apartment?

The door opens then and Thomas glances out, spots me and instantly sobers. "Oh. I heard something. Thought you were the pizza guy."

"I'm not the pizza guy," I say evenly.

"You sure aren't." He jumps forward, taking the bags from me. "Come in. I've got a surprise for you."

I can't make words come out of my mouth, but I think Thomas can see in my face I do NOT want to come in.

"We're all grown-ups," he says in a sympathetic whisper.

Just the implication that I might be acting out of immaturity is enough to send me through the door with an expression of indifference firmly in place.

Holden is sitting on the couch next to Hank Junior, who looks like manna has fallen from the sky in the form of his favorite dog treats. His chin is on Holden's knee. He glances at me with his big brown eyes, and if he could speak, his message couldn't have been any clearer. *He's back.*

Holden lifts Hank Junior's head from his knees, stands, and shoves his hands in the front pockets of his jeans. "Hi, CeCe."

"Hey, Holden." My voice goes hoarse and I clear my throat. "I didn't know you were coming to town." My tone is lemonade sweet. I so wish I could erase it and start all over.

"Kind of last minute," he says.

Thomas walks up behind me and puts a hand on my shoulder. "He's got some amazing news."

"Oh yeah?"

"Hart Holcomb is cutting "What You Took From Me" tomorrow. We just went out and met with him. It's pretty incredible how he connected with the song."

"Congratulations," I say, forcing myself to meet Holden's sober gaze. "It's an amazing song."

"Thanks."

I try to make myself look away, make an excuse about needing to put away the groceries. But my mouth won't form the words, and my feet won't obey my brain. We watch each other like two people unsure of who's going to make the first move. For a second, his guard drops, and I see in his eyes the Holden who sat outside that pound all night with me, waiting to get in and save Hank Junior. I see the Holden who kissed me that same night the way I'd always imagined being kissed; in a way I'd never been kissed before. I remember clearly how it had felt as if I'd found something I didn't know I'd been waiting for.

Just as quickly, I remember what it felt like to lose it.

"How is Sarah?" I ask.

"She's great," he says. "Actually, really great."

"That's wonderful," I say. Thomas has filled me in on her treatments, some of it good, some of it not, and I'm relieved to hear Holden say she's doing well now. "How is Patsy?"

"Bossy and opinionated," he says.

I smile at this. "What Beagle isn't?"

Holden's eyes reflect his fondness for the dog, and I'm happy for her.

"Thomas says y'all are playing all over town. Glad to hear it's going well." The words sound sincere enough, although there's a flatness there that makes me wonder if he's tried to distance himself from thoughts of it.

"We've been having fun," I say, wondering if Thomas has told him about the tour with Case.

But then Thomas says, "Yeah, about that. We've actually got some pretty cool news too, Holden. Case Phillips has asked us to replace the opening act for his tour. We've got three weeks to look like we know what the heck we're doing."

Holden's face registers surprise. "Whoa. That's amazing."

"Yeah, it is," Thomas agrees. He hesitates before adding, "Beck will be joining us."

This time the surprise in Holden's eyes is etched with something else, flashing so quickly that I can't be sure if it's admiration or regret. "Cool," he says. "I didn't know you'd been playing together."

"We haven't," I say.

"Oh," he says, as if he suddenly understands, when I'm sure he doesn't.

"Until now, it's just been CeCe and me." Thomas stops there, and then, "Now that you're here, why don't you join us? We need an electric guitar. Who better than you?"

The suggestion takes Holden as much by surprise as it does me, if the look on his face is any indication. "Hey, no. This is y'all's thing. And it's great. I'm not horning in on your action."

Thomas looks at me, trying to gauge my reaction. I don't give him one.

"Man, with the exception of Sarah, we'd have Barefoot Outlook back together. You were part of what we started here."

"And I left."

"And you're back," Thomas says.

"For good?" I say before I can stop the question from popping out.

"I don't really know yet," Holden answers.

"But what about Sarah and–" I stop and immediately apologize. "I'm sorry. That's none of my business."

"No. It's okay," Holden says. "Sarah and I are. . .we're going to be good friends."

I absorb this explanation the way I imagine a mountainside might work at absorbing a sudden deluge of rain. It is simply too much to take in so unexpectedly, and I nod once as if I understand, when I do not at all.

"Things are different now," Thomas says, in an obvious attempt to bridge a gap that cannot or will not be clearly defined at the moment. "I want you with us."

Holden and I aren't looking at each other. We both have our gazes hooked on Thomas, who's wearing a stubborn expression I recognize all too well.

"Look," he adds, "we all came here for the music. We've hit a few speed bumps and taken a couple of detours, but it still comes back to the fact that we live it, breathe it, love it. We're getting a break here with this tour. And we all know how hard those are to come by. We'll have a far better shot at going somewhere with this if you're part of it."

I let myself look at Holden, and it's clear Thomas's words mean something to him. I imagine then how it must have felt to be away from all of this for the past year and a half. To put the dream in a drawer and walk away from it, never intending to open it up again. And now. Another chance. Am I going to be the one to stand in his way? If so, what will that really accomplish?

One thing and one thing only. The protection of my own heart. My own pride. Getting over Holden, if I ever did actually reach a point where it qualified as that, took every bit of will I could scrape up from the bottom of my determination to accept something I could not change. I built a wall around my heart and told myself I never wanted to fall like that again. And I don't. The thought of being around Holden and not letting that happen is more than a little terrifying.

Even so, I remember how Holden had been against me joining up with Thomas and him when we'd first gotten to Nashville. He'd changed his mind, and I'd been grateful for the chance.

How can I be the one to close him out now?

I can't.

Not even when I'm aware of exactly how high a price I'm going to pay for making this choice.

♪

THOMAS KNOCKS ON my door at seven the next morning. I know his knock by now, and I consider pretending not to have heard it, but I lift up and mumble, "Come in."

He steps in the room, walks over and sits down on the edge of the bed. Hank Junior cracks an eye open, then puts his head back on my pillow and ignores him.

"CeCe?" Thomas says.

"Yeah?" I answer, my gaze on the wall.

"Thank you."

"For what?"

"You know what."

"I figure I owe you both for picking me up on the side of the highway."

"That was no biggie."

"Yeah, it was. I very well could have turned around and walked Hank and me back home at that point. If I believed in signs, I would have. So we're even."

"That's not a debt I would've called in."

"I know."

"I guess you also know Holden tried to do what he thought was right in going back to Atlanta to be there for Sarah. He pretty much gave up everything to do that."

I nod.

"And I know this isn't easy for you."

"I'm a big girl, Thomas. And I have someone in my life. What happened between Holden and me is part of our past. That's all."

"You sure about that?"

"Very," I say. "There is one thing though."

"What?"

"I'd like for you to be the one to tell Beck about Holden. I think it will sting less."

"Sure. We really do need him, you know. It's not like we're creating a spot for him."

I want to deny it, but the truth is we'll be lucky to have him. "We should start working today."

"As soon as we're done with the recording, I'll text you."

"Beck said we can practice at his house."

"Cool," he says, standing. "CeCe?"

"Yeah?"

"You're awesome."

"Don't forget it," I say, looking up at him with an attempt to stay stern-faced, and failing.

He leans over and kisses my cheek. "I won't," he says.

♪

Holden

"You know how you've dreamed about something for so long that it starts to feel like if it ever actually happened, it wouldn't even seem real?"

Thomas asks me the question in a low whisper while we are sitting behind Hart Holcomb's producer and a recording engineer in a Music Row studio complete with every piece of sound equipment I could ever imagine having access to. Hart is warming up inside the booth, going through parts of the song time and again, and it feels anything but real to hear him singing the words I wrote. "Yeah," I say. "That's what I'm thinking right now."

"It really is like you wrote it for him."

"Pretty sad though, you know."

"But maybe someone who hears it will think twice about having another drink and then getting behind the wheel. If one person's life is saved, that makes you a hero."

"I'm not the one who'll be selling it to people."

"No, but they're your words."

I don't say anything else because hearing Hart sing the last line makes my throat close up. With the fade of the final note, there's a collective breath blown out around the room.

"Wow, Hart," the producer says. "That's just plain powerful."

Hart clears his throat and takes a swig of water from the bottle next to him. "Thanks. And I'd like to thank Holden for writing it, y'all. He's never lived the story of this song but the way he wrote it would make you think he has. That's the mark of a great writer. I expect we'll be seeing you in big places, Holden."

Everyone is looking at me now. I don't have any idea what to say. Thomas claps me on the shoulder, and I finally manage, "Thank you so much. If this is the only song of mine that ever gets cut, I'll be all right with that. This is an honor. Really."

Hart smiles at me and through the sadness in his eyes, I glimpse a man I hope will one day know happiness again. Tragedy has clearly taken its toll on him. It's nice to think that maybe in putting out a song that might stop one person from causing the kind of pain he's known, there could be some renewal of purpose for him.

They play through it one more time before the producer says, "You ready to do it for real, Hart?"

"Ready," he says.

The studio is pin-drop quiet throughout the entire song, and I'm amazed that both Hart and the band hit every note perfectly and don't stop even once.

"Whoa," Thomas says when they're done. "Pretty impressive," I say.

By the time they lay the background vocals, it's after four o'clock. Just as the producer declares it a wrap, a guy in a jacket and jeans walks into the studio, speaks for a moment with Hart and then comes over to where Thomas and I are getting up to go.

He says hello to Thomas and sticks his hand out to me. "You must be Holden. I'm Andrew Seeger, Hart's manager. I hear things went incredibly well today."

"It was amazing to watch," I say.

"I'm glad it's all worked out." He reaches inside his jacket and pulls out a folded pack of papers. "Sorry I didn't get this over sooner but this is our standard contract. I believe you'll find the terms extremely appealing. As I'm sure you've already figured out, Hart really wanted this song."

I unfold the papers and glance through the first page, my eyes widening at the numbers there. "Wow. That's. . .thank you."

"We're expecting big things from this. Get ready. I think you're going to be amazed by the number of knocks you'll be getting on your door."

"Thank you," I say again, because I have no idea what else to add. I sign my name on the places he indicates I should sign. We shake hands and then I walk over and thank Hart again.

Thomas and I say nothing until we're in his truck and pulling out of the parking lot.

"Did that just happen?" Thomas asks.

"As far as I can tell, it was real."

"Dang."

"Yeah."

"You're gonna be famous."

"Shut up."

Thomas grins. "Don't go all modest. You earned it. It's a great song."

"Thanks, but luck has to play some part in it. You think I ever imagined something like this?"

"No," Thomas interrupts. "I don't. You still deserve it."

"You're a good friend, Thomas," I say, suddenly serious and wishing I knew how to say how much it means to me that any success either one of us has is never ruined by resentment or jealousy.

"Speaking of which," he segues, "I called Beck when you were talking with Hart after we first got to the studio."

"How'd that go?" I ask, suddenly sure I know what the answer will be.

"He was totally cool with it," Thomas says. "I gotta say, it's not what I was expecting."

"That's kind of a surprise."

"Just so you know, I don't think he's worried about you sweeping CeCe off her feet."

I consider this, weigh my conflicting responses and decide on, "He doesn't need to be."

"Doesn't he?" Thomas asks, looking over at me, dead serious.

"No."

"Can we have an honest moment here?"

"Thomas, I–"

"Hear me out, okay. I think it needs to be said." He taps a thumb against the steering wheel and then goes on with, "It took a long time for CeCe to start acting like herself again. You put a pretty big dent in her heart, friend."

There's no criticism in the statement, just flat truth. "I never meant to hurt her," I say.

"I know. If we're playing together, maybe it really would be best for things to stay the way they are. Everybody knows it's difficult for groups to stay together. And for whatever reason, Case wants Beck in on this gig. War between you two would pretty much dump the whole thing in the landfill."

"Thanks, friend."

"You can't deny it, can you?"

I want to but I actually don't think I can. "No," I say.

"It seems like Beck is good to her," Thomas says, clearly not enjoying this.

"That's good."

"It really is." He looks out the window as if thinking twice about what he's about to say. "You two could have been really good together. There's a lot of water under that particular bridge, and I'd hate to see either one of you-"

"Drown?"

"Something like that."

"You don't need to say anything else. I get it."

"Then why do I feel like such a jerk?"

♪

WE GET TO BECK'S place just as an enormous storm cloud breaks open and dumps rain so fast and hard that the driveway looks like a small river. We pull in at the front of the house behind a BMW. Beck slides out of the driver's side and runs around with an umbrella to open the passenger door. CeCe gets out and ducks under it, laughing as they run inside.

I watch them with a sense of loss that I know I have no right to feel. But it's there anyway, like a kick to the gut.

"You sure you're gonna be able to do this?" Thomas asks.

"I'm good," I say, the question prodding me to slide out of the truck. I grab my guitar case from its spot between us. Thomas walks around, and I follow him to the door. He rings the bell.

The door swings open, and Beck says, "Y'all get in out of the rain."

"Hey, man," Thomas says, walking inside.

I walk in behind him and stick a hand out to Beck. "Hey. Good to see you again."

"You too," Beck says with what looks like a genuine smile. "Glad it worked out that you can hook up with us on the tour. Dad was psyched about it."

"Thanks," I say. "I really appreciate the chance to be here." I want to be suspicious of his friendliness. I mean, why would he want me back here? If I were him, I wouldn't let me within fifty miles of CeCe. But then, maybe he's that confident of what they have going.

We follow him through the long hallway that I remember as leading to his dad's studio. CeCe is already there, warming up when we walk in. I haven't heard her sing since leaving here – correction – haven't let myself hear her sing since leaving here. Her voice has taken on new dimension and power. She sounds amazing.

She smiles at Beck and Thomas but stops short of meeting eyes with me. "Y'all ready to do this thing?"

"Let's jump on it," Thomas says. "Should we go through a playlist first?"

"Sure," Beck says.

"CeCe and I can highlight the songs we've been doing. Holden, you got any good new stuff?"

"I've got new stuff. Not sure if it's any good or not."

"Check the modesty," Thomas says. "Ladies and gents, you're looking at Hart Holcomb's prediction for one of this town's up and coming hit songwriters."

Both Beck and CeCe glance at me with a look of surprise. It's CeCe who speaks first.

"So it went well?"

"Yeah," I say. "He's an incredible singer."

"Congratulations," Beck says. "That's big stuff. Sounds like you've impressed him. I've heard my dad say that's not an easy thing to do."

"I think I got a lucky break," I say. "Right song. Right place."

We all pull up a chair at the round table in one corner of the room. From there, we start talking about songs, compiling a list of the best we have and then working out the playlist.

Beck knows all of the songs CeCe and Thomas have been singing from having been at so many of their shows. They ask me to play some of my new stuff. I put my thoughts on the individual songs and try not to think about the fact that Beck has entwined his fingers with CeCe's as if she's just been taken under by an unexpected current and it is up to him to save her.

And I wonder if he's that sure of her, after all.

♪

CeCe

We spend the next five hours practicing song after song, perfecting some Thomas and I already know well and then working on several new ones Holden says he wrote over the past year.

The songs are really good, and I'm relieved to see that he has continued to write. Our upbeat songs outnumber the ballads six to one, and we all agree that as the opening act, we want to get the audience up and ready to have a good time.

At first, I'm so nervous that I forget lines to songs I know by heart. I actually feel every single time Holden glances at me, but I manage not to look back. I know it's crazy. After all, how can I expect to get through an entire tour without looking at him? Whatever it is holding in place all of my determination to make this work feels about as fragile as baby grass under an April frost.

It's almost ten when we call it a wrap. I'm as tired from the effort of smiling and trying to act normal as I am from the rehearsing.

Once we've packed up all our things, Beck says he'll take me home.

"We're headed back to the apartment, CeCe, if you want to ride with us," Thomas offers.

I don't want to but it would be a little silly for Beck to drive all the way into town just to drop me off. And since I'm too tired to do anything other than go to bed, going out isn't an option. "Okay," I say. "That will save you a trip, Beck."

"I'm happy to take you."

I hear the edge in his voice and know we will end up talking about things I don't want to talk about right now. I take the coward's way out. "I'll see you tomorrow. Call me in the morning?"

"Sure." He walks over to kiss me full on the mouth. He takes his time in a statement to Holden. I start to pull away, but force myself not to. Can I blame him for feeling insecure? Wouldn't I, if the circumstances were reversed?

I wait for him to end the kiss and press my palm to his cheek. "Please tell your dad thank you for letting us rehearse here."

"I will," he says. "Goodnight."

"'Night," I say and follow Thomas and Holden from the room.

In the truck, I sit to the left of the middle so that my shoulder is touching Thomas's, putting two inches of space between Holden and me.

"I thought it went great," Thomas says as he pulls out of the long driveway onto the main road headed back to the city. "What did you two think?"

Neither of us answers for a few moments, both obviously waiting the other out. I give first.

"We've got some polishing to do, but I like where we're going."

"I agree," Holden says, his gaze set outside the window.

"CeCe, I really like what you did with the bridge on that last song. That's gonna get you a lot of fans, girl."

"Thanks, Thomas," I say, feeling a familiar tenderness toward him. If anyone in this world has my back now, it's Thomas.

We talk about different issues we need to address with certain parts of the songs. It makes the drive go quickly and keeps me from focusing on how close I am to touching Holden.

At the apartment, I take Hank Junior for a walk and deliberately stay out long enough that I hope to avoid seeing Holden again tonight. Hank sniffs every tree we pass and protests my turning back toward home by locking his legs and giving me a visual declaration of his displeasure.

"Come on," I say. "You'd stay out here all night if I let you."

To make up for not letting him have his way, I give him a cookie when we get back inside. He wags his tail in forgiveness and licks my hand.

"I see he still knows how to work the system."

I jump at the sound of Holden's voice and turn to look at him with what I hope comes across as mild interest. "I try not to let him get too big a head."

"Kind of a benevolent dictator, isn't he?"

It pretty much nails Hank's role in life, and I can't stop myself from smiling. "Sadly, I don't mind."

"He has that effect, doesn't he?"

I nod, making a pretense of wiping crumbs off the kitchen counter and putting the treat jar back in place. "Thomas already in bed?"

"Yeah. I think we wore him out."

"Well," I say, "I'm tired too. Goodnight, Holden."

I start past him, Hank Junior at my heels. Holden reaches out and stops me with a hand on my arm. "CeCe?"

I stop, as if instantly frozen in place. I try to say something but my voice is locked in my throat.

"Can we talk for a minute?" he asks.

"About what?" I finally manage. "There isn't anything-"

"Actually, there is."

"Holden-"

"Please."

I force myself to turn and face him then, saying nothing, waiting for him to go on.

"I want to say I'm sorry for everything that happened."

His eyes are fully sincere and something in me gives a little. "You have nothing to be sorry for," I say.

"I didn't mean to hurt you."

"I know." And I really do. "We never should have. . .we were wrong to-"

"*I* was wrong to," he finishes for me. "I wasn't free to let myself have feelings for you."

With those words, the urge to cry hits me so hard and so insistently that the tears are spilling from my eyes before I even try to hold them back. "Holden, don't," I say. "This is not a place either of us can afford to go."

"I still need to say it."

"Is that what's most important then?" I ask on a flurry of anger. "What you need?"

He blinks once but not fast enough to hide the flash of hurt. "That's not what I meant," he says.

"Maybe not," I say quickly. "What I need is to forget that we ever felt anything more than friendship for each other. That is the only way I can be on a stage with you every night for six weeks."

I turn abruptly then and start out of the kitchen for my room. Holden reaches out and reels me back to him. I stop only after hitting the wall of his chest.

I look up at him just as outrage surges through me. "Don't. Touch. Me. Holden."

But he doesn't remove his hand from my arm. With his gaze locked on mine, he gently pulls me forward until I am fully encircled in his embrace. I hold myself as if I have been cast in ice.

We stand that way for countless seconds. The refrigerator hums. The air conditioning kicks on. A cat meows somewhere outside and Hank Junior pads over to the window to investigate.

And then, slowly, slowly, Holden eases me in, folding me into the circle of his arms until I just melt against him.

Everything inside of me goes liquid and warm. I close my eyes and yield to the irresistible need to breathe him in, to let myself remember how I feel magnetized next to him. Completely unable to resist the pull between us.

I want to protest. My brain is telling me to protest. But my body isn't listening.

Instead, I let my arms wrap him up and I press my face to his chest. His warm, hard chest. Time falls away. I don't let myself think of anything except what is here, what is now.

He puts his cheek against my hair, and I feel him sigh, a release of breath, as if he, too, has been holding it since the last time we were in each other's arms like this.

We stay this way for a very long while. I can feel the pain and hurt of these past eighteen months absorb into the air around us and fade to acceptance.

"What was it like?" I ask, my voice little more than a whisper.

"What?" he answers, the question rough at the edges.

"Seeing her go through all of that."

"Terrifying." He's quiet for several moments and then, "I never imagined so many people having their lives destroyed by that awful disease. Going with her to the treatments, seeing others who were even sicker than she was . . . some days, I didn't think I could go back."

"It must have been hard," I say softly.

"Seeing the hope and courage of those people, and how fragile it all is, I swear, sometimes I wanted to change places with them just so their hopes weren't for nothing."

Tears fill my eyes. I bite my lower lip before saying, "I'm sorry."

"I saw things that made me realize what I take for granted in my life. Little kids who'd lost all their hair, who couldn't eat. And their parents, trying to act if everything would be all right."

He stops there, and I can feel his grief like a wall that is crumbling inside him. I tighten my arms around his waist and hold onto him as if I am the only thing that will keep him from collapsing under its weight.

I'm not sure how much time passes with the two of us standing here, holding each other. I wish that we never had to move, that we could stay like this forever.

But I know we can't; there are people in our lives who have not asked to be hurt by us. I ease away from him, looking up into his eyes. "Sarah. She's going to be okay?"

"I think so," Holden says. "The doctors have said she's clear, and she works at the nutrition end of it. Really at doing anything she can to stay healthy."

"I'm glad," I say, and with this picture of her, I step back, loosen my hold on him. "Will she . . . is she planning to move here?"

He doesn't say anything for a few moments and I start to wonder if I've asked more than I should have.

"No," he says then. "Sarah and I, we're not going to be together."

The admission takes me by such surprise that I am sure I must have misheard him. "Oh. I thought. . .what?"

"We're not."

"But why?"

He looks away and then back at me. "Maybe she saw us through new eyes and didn't like what was there."

I don't know what to say so I don't say anything.

"There was something else," he adds. "She met someone who might have made her realize what she did want."

"Holden. I. . .I'm sorry."

"Don't be. I'm pretty sure she's going to be happy. That's what matters."

I take in the words with a feeling of disbelief. And all of a sudden, I feel the dissolving of a barrier between us. With it comes an awkwardness I have no idea what to do with. "I don't know what to say, Holden."

"You don't have to say anything, CeCe. You've moved on. I get it. I understand. And I'm not here to mess up things with you and Beck."

I know I should feel relieved. Because he's right. I have moved on. It took a long time but I've moved on. And now someone else's heart is involved. *Beck's* heart is involved. *My* heart is involved.

There's no unraveling all of that. Even if I wanted to.

"I'm sorry, Holden. For everything you've been through. For-"

He places a fingertip against my lips and says, "Shh. It's okay. We'll be okay. All of us."

And I want to believe him. I really do. I'm just not sure how to start.

♪

FOR THE NEXT three weeks, we practice as hard as I've ever imagined working. Thomas and I give notice at our jobs and, thankfully, neither place insists that we work it out. When Thomas asks me if I'm okay with Holden moving back in, I have no good reason to say no. He drives to Atlanta two days after our talk in the kitchen and arrives back in a rental car twenty-four hours later with Patsy in the front seat next to him.

Hank Junior is so happy to see her I don't think he quits wagging his tail for a week. He follows her everywhere, as if he's afraid if he lets her out of his sight, she'll disappear again.

We rehearse twelve to fourteen hours a day, polishing our performance until we're nailing every song, word for word, note for note.

And for those three weeks, Holden is right about everything being okay. No one has time to think about anything other than eating, sleeping, and getting ready for the tour. When we get home every night, I fall in bed and sleep like Rip Van Winkle.

My biggest worry is what to do with Hank Junior when we're gone. Since Holden has the same concern about Patsy, he, Thomas and I brainstorm options one morning while we're waiting for Beck in his dad's studio.

"We can't leave them in a kennel for six weeks," Holden says, taking a sip from the coffee the housekeeper, Nelda, made for us when we arrived.

Thomas makes a choking sound. "Yeah, right. CeCe would check *herself* into a kennel for six weeks before she'd leave Hank there."

I raise an eyebrow at him but there's no point in denying the accusation. We all know it's true.

Beck walks in, his hair still wet from the shower. He kisses me on the cheek and says, "What's up with the pow-wow?"

"Just trying to figure out what we're going to do with Hank Junior and Patsy while we're away." I hear the worry in my own voice because with every passing day, I'm more stressed by my lack of a solution.

Beck sits down next to me and pours a cup of coffee. "They could stay here with Nelda."

I lean back and look at him, not sure if he means it. "Are you serious?"

"Yeah," he says. "She loves dogs."

"But what about your dad?"

"He won't mind. They'll give Nelda someone to cook for. When dad's gone anyone left here gets overfed and then some."

"That would be amazing," I say, leaning forward to give him a hug.

Holden gets up from the table to pour another cup of coffee, his back to us. "That's incredibly nice. Thanks, man. Really."

"No skin," Beck says.

"All right then," Thomas says. "Let's get to work."

♪

Holden

The tour begins in San Francisco. Three days on the bus across country, and we're all ready to be there. I've spent most of those miles trying to focus on anything but the fact that Beck can't keep his hands off CeCe.

I get a lot of reading done.

Keeping my eyes on the page and my head in someone else's story is about the only distraction that works.

We arrive in the city on the morning of the first show. After grabbing a few hours of sleep in an actual bed, we leave for the venue where we can practice on stage and get a feel for the acoustics.

The place feels absolutely enormous. We've never played anywhere that would hold half this many people, and looking out at the thousands of empty chairs, I start to wonder if we're really up for this.

"I see what you're thinking." Thomas walks up behind me and claps a hand on my shoulder. "No reason to go there now."

"This could be a major fail," I say.

"Glass half-full, please."

"Don't tell me you're not wondering what we were thinking."

"Okay, so the thought crossed my mind," he concedes. "But we're here. We've done our homework."

"Could I get an infusion of some of your confidence, please?"

Thomas snorts. "Since when do you need confidence?"

"Since we decided we could pull off opening a show for a country music legend."

"We can. Have you heard us?" He pulls his iPhone out of his shirt pocket, swipes the screen, taps it twice and one of our songs begins playing. Thomas waits a minute and then it turns it off. "That sound good or what?"

I have to admit we sound pretty good. "Let's just hope we hit that tonight."

"Faith, man. Where's your faith?"

"Working on it."

"Stay away from CeCe until you get it in place. She's already a bundle of nerves."

Just then, she and Beck walk onstage. She looks as serious as I've ever seen her. She bites her lower lip and glances out at the sea of seats in front of the stage. Her eyes widen.

"Okay," Thomas says. "I think it's time for a pep talk. Y'all get on over here."

He waves us to the end of the stage. We all sit down in a line, facing out to where all those faces will be looking at CeCe and me, and Beck on her other side.

"Anyone here dreamed about this as long as I have?" Thomas asks.

No one says anything for a few moments, and then CeCe admits, "Yes."

Her voice has a tremble in it. Thomas reaches over and covers her hand with his.

"Anyone else?"

"Yeah," I say.

Thomas looks at Beck. "How about you?"

"I've pretty much wanted to be my dad for as long as I can remember," he says in a low voice.

The admission surprises me. It's not something I would expect a guy like Beck to say.

"So, okay," Thomas says. "We all agree this is important to us. And we don't want to screw it up. The only way that's going to happen is if we forget we're anywhere other than at home in Nashville, practicing the way we've been practicing for weeks. We've got this. Y'all know we do. Every song. Every word. Every note. We've got it. Right?"

No one says anything for a long string of moments. Somewhere behind the stage, I hear equipment being unloaded from the tractor-trailer trucks. The whine of a forklift. The clank of metal cases. Conversation and laughter from the guys working hard and fast to get it all in.

CeCe draws in a deep breath and says, "We've got it."

"Beck?" Thomas says.

"Yeah, man. We've got it."

My best friend looks at me, one eyebrow raised.
"We've got it," I say. "We've got it."

♪

CeCe

I am so scared I actually feel my knees trembling.

Two minutes until we're out there in front of thousands of Case Phillips fans, who will pretty much decide with the first song whether we're worthy of being on this tour or not.

My heart is pounding so hard I feel its throb like a bass drum in my ears. I wish with everything inside me that my mama could be here tonight. It's not that I don't understand why she isn't. She's terrified of flying, and driving across country isn't something I can imagine her doing. She'll be at the show in Annapolis, Maryland, and that's good enough. That doesn't make me crave one of her reassuring hugs right now any less though.

The four of us are standing to the side of the stage and we're all wearing varying expressions of "Is this really happening?"

The crowd tonight is two thousand or so, one of the smaller venues for the tour, but the largest by far I've ever sung in front of.

"I'm not sure I can do this," I say. Only then do I realize I've said it out loud.

Holden steps up and dips his head in close to mine. "Where's a place you've sung that made you the happiest?" he asks, his voice low and calming.

I don't turn to look at him. I lace my hands together in front of me and think hard. The memory, when it comes, is sweet and poignant. "In church on the Sunday my granny was baptized. She was eighty-three. She asked the pastor if I could do a solo of "Just As I Am"."

"Yeah?"

I nod, letting myself remember what a wonderful day that had been. "By that point, she couldn't walk very well, and it took a lot of courage for her to step down into that water. Watching her and singing the words to that song at the same time made me understand what it really meant. I was so proud to have been a part of that day."

"Don't you think she'd be proud of you now?" he asks in a low voice.

I let my gaze meet his. "I do," I say softly.

"Then think about that tonight when you're out there singing. Nothing else but that."

"Thanks, Holden," I say, and for a moment, just a moment, I let myself remember why I fell in love with him so quickly. This way he has of anchoring me in the middle of a storm I am sure is big enough to overtake me. I trust him to know the way, to lead me out. I can't explain the why of it. I just know it's true.

"Welcome to the San Francisco Bayside Coliseum and the Case Phillips' Brand New Me Tour!"

The announcer's shout-out is loud enough to soften the roar of the crowd.

"This is one ticket you're going to be so glad you bought. First out tonight, a new group Case has been talking up all over Nashville, and when you hear them, you'll understand why! Folks, let's give a big California welcome to Barefoot Outlook!"

"Yee-haw!" Thomas whoops. "Here we go, y'all!"

He leads me across the stage, one fist pounding the air, the other hand clasped in mine as if he knows there's a good chance I'll run. From the corner of my eye, I see Beck and Holden taking their places, picking up their guitars.

Thomas and I reach for our microphones, and he dips into the first song of our set – "What We Feel." I wrote this song and I know it like I know my own face in the mirror. I'm supposed to come in on the chorus but my mind has gone completely blank. I know what Thomas is going to sing before I hear the words but I can't think of how the first line of the chorus begins. He's into the pre-chorus now. I feel the impending arrival of my turn to join in like a roller coaster about to reach the top of the first hill, aware that the bottom is going to fall out at any second.

My face feels frozen and I can't make myself smile. Thomas glances over at me, his eyes questioning. I know he wants to help. There's nothing he can do.

Someone steps up behind me just then, puts an arm around my shoulders, and I realize it's Case. I'm sure he's going to signal me off the stage, take my place, but he starts into the chorus with Thomas, still holding onto me.

The crowd erupts at the sound of his voice, screaming and whooping their surprise at his appearance.

And suddenly the words are coming back to me. Case must feel my relief because he shouts out, "CeCe McKenzie, folks, this girl's got couuuuntry!"

And as if he's just handed me the baton in a relay race, I swoop into the second verse with the same level of confidence I had reached during our rehearsals of this song.

The audience begins to clap and stomp out the rhythm as I go, and all of a sudden, I'm having more fun than I've ever had on stage. My heart feels like it might burst with gratitude for Case's generosity.

He joins us on the chorus again.

It's what we feel
That makes the memories
It's what we feel
That gives us history
The part that's real
It's what we feel

Thomas and I take the bridge, and then all three of us finish it out. At the end, Case kisses my cheek and heads off the stage. The audience is cheering so loudly, I'm not sure they can even hear the beginning of our next song. But it doesn't matter, I know every word. I sing like I've never sung before, giving it heart, mind, soul, me.

♪

AFTER THE SHOW, we sign autographs for fans who received back stage passes through Case's fan club. It's a little shocking to see the line of people extending down the hallway outside the room where we're having a buffet supper set up by a catering company.

The crowd is mostly made up of girls, a few guys here and there who are most likely boyfriends forced to come along. Thomas,

Holden, Beck and I are at the start of the line. Case is at the other end so that the fans get to him last.

A young girl who looks to be about thirteen holds out a t-shirt for me to sign. The front says Brand New Me Tour. The back reads Case Phillips and Barefoot Outlook. Every time I see that, my stomach drops as if released from elevator cables.

How we got here, I am still not sure.

"Your voice is amazing," the girl says, looking up at me with an awe I don't see myself ever getting used to. "I could listen to you all night."

"Thank you so much," I say, smiling at her.

"I sing too," she says.

"That's wonderful. What do you like to sing?"

"Anything I can get anybody to listen to," she admits with a shy smile. "My daddy says I could sing the stripes off a zebra."

I laugh. "That's some awfully good singing."

"Not as good as you though. How long did it take you to sound like you do?"

"I started when I was really young, like you," I say. "If it's what you love to do, it's not even work. For me, I was just always happy to be doing it. Anytime. Anywhere."

Thomas elbows me. "Hey, how about saving a fan or two for me?"

The girl giggles and says to Thomas, "You're really good too, you know."

"Thank you, ma'am," he says, bestowing a smile on her that lights her cheeks up to apple red. He signs her shirt as well and when she's moved on to where Beck is standing next to his dad, I shake my head at him.

"What?" he asks, grinning.

"You're a natural at this," I say.

"I like making people smile."

"You sure can do that." I glance around the room, not for the first time since we've been standing here, and add, "Where is Holden?"

"Said he was going to take a shower."

"He should be signing too."

"He's not much on this part," Thomas says. "Never has been."

I'm not surprised by this but it still doesn't seem right that he's not out here taking some of the credit.

A very tall guy with white-blonde hair stops in front of me and holds out a ticket stub. He looks to be in his late twenties or so. "Could you sign this please?" he asks, his voice smooth, polite.

Smiling, I look up at him. His eyes are the lightest blue I've ever seen. He's smiling back at me but something in his expression makes me instantly want to take a step back. I have to force myself not to. He's looking at me as if he can see right through me. I actually feel goose bumps shiver across my arms.

"I . . . sure," I say, taking the ticket and writing, "Happiness is a Barefoot Outlook. CeCe."

He reads it and smiles again. I can't explain what it is about him, some weird energy or maybe just my imagination. The way he's staring at me feels off somehow.

"Looks like you're living the dream. Touring with Case Phillips. That's big stuff."

I feel my heart thump an inexplicable note of alarm. "We're all grateful to be here," I say.

"You're out of Nashville, right?"

I nod. "Yes." I try to make eye contact with Thomas but he's talking with someone and not looking my way. Neither is Beck or Case.

"How long before you got your break?"

I start to ask what he means but I don't want to lengthen the conversation so I say, "I've been there almost two years."

"Two years? Is that all?" He laughs. "I'd like to get your recipe for success."

Panic flutters through me now and I am certain I need to move away from him. A hand grasps my arm and I jump before I realize it's Holden. He steps halfway in front of me. The adrenaline of instant relief pumps outward from my chest.

"Hey," the guy says with a sarcastic lilt.

Holden now turns fully toward him, standing in between us. "You should move on."

"Should I?"

"You should."

"What happens if I don't?"

"I happen." Holden's voice is steel.

The guy raises both hands in concession, still holding the ticket I signed. "Chill, dude. You go ballistic every time somebody chats up your chick?"

Holden steps forward, forcing him to move back. Case's two bodyguards, John and Miles, are now walking toward us, both hulking weightlifters whose muscle is not for show.

"Everything okay here?" John asks, looking directly at the guy.

"I was just leaving," he says, the words now as neutral as his expression.

"Why don't we walk you out?" Miles says in a voice that makes it clear his offer isn't a suggestion.

He gives me one last look, his eyes lit with amusement, before turning to walk toward the door with them.

I turn and head for the dressing room, my pace fast and uneven, my knees so shaky I think they might actually collapse beneath me. I am aware of Holden following me but I don't stop until I reach the room with my name on it.

He walks in behind me. "Are you okay, CeCe?"

"Will you close it? And lock it? Please."

He does as I ask, concern on his face. "Hey. You're okay."

I sit on the small sofa against one wall, managing a nod, shivering. "What did he say?"

I shake my head. "It was more like the way he said it."

Holden sits down beside me and slowly pulls me into the curve of his arm. "He's gone. Everything is all right."

I nod, forcing myself to focus on those two words and their ability to melt my panic.

"He really freaked you out," Holden says, smoothing the back of his hand across my hair. "I admit he was a little creepy, but is there something else going on?"

I want to tell him, except it's been so long since I've let myself think about any of it that I'm not sure I can bring it to life again with words. "I . . . had a bad experience a few years ago. I guess he reminded me of it."

Holden studies me for a moment and then says, "What happened, CeCe?"

I look down and rub my thumb against the back of one hand. "It was right after I first started going on the road. Weekend stuff. I began noticing this man showing up in the audience, even when the shows were in different places, hours apart. At first, he just watched me and never approached me. But then he began sitting at a front table, and throughout the entire show, he wouldn't take his eyes off me."

"Did you call the police?"

"At that point, I didn't have anything to report. I started to see him in other places. At the grocery store. Parked outside my high school when I got there in the mornings. He even came to my house one night when Mama was at church. I heard a knock and opened the door before I realized-"

I break off there because my voice is shaking and I can't get the rest of the words out.

Holden puts his arm around me and pulls me into the curve of his shoulder. I hold myself rigid for a few moments but then I close my eyes and sink against him, remembering how safe I feel there.

"Did he hurt you?" he asks, his voice low and laced with anger.

I shake my head. "I was able to slam the door and call the police. There was nothing to arrest him for at that point."

"What else did he do?"

"Punctured the tires on Mama's car when I borrowed it one night to go to a show in Raleigh. Surveillance cameras proved that he did it."

"Did he go to jail?"

"For ninety days."

"That's it?" he asks, sounding disgusted.

I nod.

"Has he bothered you since?"

"While he was in jail, someone would call our house and hang up. Eventually, that stopped, and I haven't heard from him again."

"You're sure this isn't the same guy?"

"I'm sure."

We sit, quiet for a good while before he says, "I don't want you to go anywhere by yourself, okay?"

"I won't."

"He's probably some jokester with a bad sense of humor, but there's no reason to take a chance."

I pull back a bit and look up at him. "Thank you," I say.

"For what?"

"Being there."

"I'm glad I was."

He brushes his hand across my cheek, and just that light touch snags something low inside me that responds to him in a way I've never responded to anyone else. My breathing goes instantly shallow.

"You're beautiful, CeCe."

The words are like the lick of a flame along my skin, and I hear in his voice that he knows he shouldn't have said them.

"I really want you to kiss me," I say softly, deliberately.

"I really want to kiss you," he says, equally soft, equally deliberate.

I lean in a little closer. There's a moment of hesitation in us both. He answers my invitation so suddenly and with such intensity that I forget to breathe, forget everything except the instant memory of how his lips feel against mine. Heated and knowing, familiar and skilled.

I slide my palms up the expanse of his hard-muscled abs and chest, the ripples and contours clearly defined beneath the thin cotton of his t-shirt. Touching him, molding myself to him, it's almost impossible to believe I'm not dreaming. Because I've dreamed this dream so many times, only to wake up to daylight and the fact that I would never be held by him like this again, kissed by him like this again.

I feel the tears seeping from beneath my closed lids. I will them to stop, but they don't, they won't.

Holden pulls back and brushes his thumb across my cheek. "Do you want me to quit?" he asks, instantly remorseful.

I shake my head, looking down because I can't make myself meet his gaze.

"But you're crying."

"I know," I whisper.

"Baby, why?" he says, the question sounding as if it has been torn from him.

I do let myself look at him now, and I answer as honestly as I can. "Because I've missed you so much. Because I thought we would never be together like this—"

I don't finish. He is suddenly kissing me into silence. And I am kissing him back. His hands slide under the skirt of my dress and around my bottom to lift me onto his lap so that I am straddling him, my arms winding around his neck and holding him tight. There is no space between us, one heart pounding into the other. And I think if I could melt myself into him, I would. I don't ever want to feel again what it's like to know this and lose it.

Call it weakness. Call it acceptance of something I can't change, but whatever I call it, I can't deny it.

I run my hands through his hair, kiss one eyelid and then the other, nip his chin with my teeth before sinking my mouth onto his again.

And we kiss without thought of time or any other measuring stick of the world outside this room. I don't want to think past the next moment, the next sensation spiraling through me, lifting me up and out of myself to a place where there is only this, only us.

"Do you have any idea what you do to me?" he asks, dropping his head against the back of the sofa, his eyes hazed with the same need I feel.

"I know what you do to me," I say. "I know that I've never felt this way with anyone but you."

"CeCe. I promised myself I wouldn't get between you and Beck," he says, the words infused with apology. "Tell me to get up and leave, and I will."

"I wish I could," I say, hearing the broken note in my admission. "I don't want to hurt him. I never wanted—"

"Me? Is that about right?"

I go completely still at the sound of Beck's voice, closing my eyes in the hope that I imagined it.

Holden gently slides me off his lap, stands, and pulls me to my feet. We both face Beck with solemn expressions.

"Beck . . . man, we didn't mean for this to happen," Holden says. "It wasn't planned."

Beck shoves a hand through his hair and laughs, a harsh sound that I don't recognize in him. "There's fool and then there's Fool with a capital F. I guess that's me."

"Beck," I say. "Don't. It's not like that."

"What is it like, CeCe?" he asks, and I see the tears shining in his eyes.

My heart twists. I really hate myself for hurting him this way. "I don't know how to explain it."

"Maybe like this," he says with an edge in his voice. "Girl likes boy. Boy dumps girl. Girl tries to get over him with sucker boy. But that didn't work, did it?"

"Beck-"

"Don't bother, CeCe," he says. "I already know the ending to this story." He turns and leaves the room, slamming the door behind him so that the thin walls rattle with the force.

I sink onto the sofa, wondering exactly what I've just done.

Holden sits down next to me. "Do you want me to go after him?"

"No. It should be me. I need to talk to him."

"I don't want you alone with him when he's angry at you."

"It's okay. That's not Beck."

"How do you know?" he asks.

"I just do," I say, and then because the guilt is starting to choke me, I add, "You should go."

He watches me while weighing his decision. "I'm not leaving you alone right now."

"I'm fine. I . . . I need some time to think."

I can see that he wants to disagree but he finally relents with, "I'll check in on you in a little while. Are you sure you'll be okay?"

I nod.

He stands then without touching me again. He walks to the door, turns, and looks at me. His eyes are solemn and serious. "Do you want me to go back to pretending that I don't love you, CeCe?"

The question echoes from my head to my heart. I am at once joyful and stricken.

He loves me.
Oh.
He loves me.
"No," I say. "I don't."

♪

CeCe

I don't sleep.

I try, but the effort amounts to nothing more than rumpled sheets and a comforter that ends up on the floor.

My thoughts bounce back and forth. From Holden and loving every moment of being in his arms, to Beck and the look on his face when he walked in the room.

I feel horrible, and I really don't know where to begin to try and fix this. There is no fixing it. I can't erase what happened or the fact that I've hurt Beck in the process.

All I can do is apologize.

I give up the fight and get out of bed at four-thirty, heading for the shower where I stand under the spray for a good twenty minutes. I brush my teeth and dry my hair, slide into jeans and a t-shirt. I make myself wait until five-thirty before walking to Beck's room. It's still an indecent hour to wake anyone up but I can't wait any longer.

He's one floor down from mine. I take the elevator and get off, glancing at the number signs and turning right.

I hear the music from the far end of the hallway. It's blasting loud enough that I wonder how anybody can be sleeping.

It's not until I've almost reached his door that I realize the music is coming from his room. I stop instantly and decide this is a very bad idea. Just then, a girl stumbles backwards out of the doorway. She is laughing so hard she's holding her stomach, and she's having extreme difficulty staying upright on her stiletto heels.

"If three isn't a crowd, Beck Phillips," she says, her voice slightly slurred, "four is just getting the party started." She laughs as if she has nailed the best punch line ever.

I start to back away. She looks around and points at me, staring for a moment as if she's trying to focus. "Oh, my gosh! You're CeCe. Beck's singer. I mean, girlfriend."

I decide that now is the time to go. But she moves surprisingly fast for someone who would no doubt blow a DUI test. She lurches forward and grabs my hand, pulling me toward the room and then through the half open door.

I stop as if I have hit a concrete wall.

Beck and two girls are in the king-size bed that takes up the middle of the floor. One girl is sitting on top of him, naked. The other girl, also naked, is draped alongside him, one leg entwined with his.

He looks at me, and I can see that he's trying to focus, as if I am very far away, when actually it's only a few feet. "CeCe? Is that you?"

His words are every bit as slurred as those of the girl who pulled me into the room. His eyes are like slits, and he's clearly having trouble keeping them open.

I spot the traces of white powder on the coffee table and the two empty gin bottles.

I've never seen Beck with drugs, never known him to even want to be around anyone messing with them.

I start to back away as he says, "Did you think I'd just come down here and cry myself to sleep, CeCe?"

I shake my head, stung by the harsh tone in his voice.

"Or maybe you thought it was okay for you to screw around as long as I didn't know about it?"

"Beck. Please."

He vaults off the bed and stumbles to a stop in front of me, wearing black briefs and nothing else. The girls are giggling now, watching us the way they might an episode of their favorite sitcom.

He grabs my arms, holding onto me so tightly that I'm not sure if it's because he doesn't want me to go or if it's the only way he can keep himself upright.

"What did I do wrong?" he asks, staggering backwards a few inches and then swaying forward again. He rights himself when his chest bumps my shoulder.

"Nothing," I say. "Let's not do this now. I'll come back when you-"

"Don't have company?" he interrupts, waving a hand at the girls on the bed. "What's wrong with me having company? It's not like I have a girlfriend or anything."

I swing around to leave, certain now that things are only going to go downhill from here. But he whirls me back, and I collide with his bare chest, grabbing his arm to keep from falling.

I look up at him then, and my growing anger instantly deflates at the look in his eyes. The hurt I see there takes my breath away. "Beck. Oh, Beck. I'm sorry. I didn't mean to-"

"Break my heart?" he finishes softly. "Well, you did."

"Come back to bed, honey," one of the girls says, patting the mattress. "We were just about to fix it for you."

He reaches out and brushes my cheek with his knuckles. "I loved you, CeCe. No. I *love* you."

Regret forms a knot in my throat. I try to say something. The words won't come. I realize I don't have any that will make this better. "I'm sorry, Beck. I never wanted to hurt you."

"But you have. Right?"

I look down at my hands, unable to respond.

"You can't make your heart feel something it doesn't feel."

"Beck, I didn't plan tonight. I didn't expect it."

"Didn't want it?"

I start to respond. I realize I can't answer this without hurting him further. Because I *did* want it.

When I don't say anything, he raises a hand and drops onto the bed, sliding back in between the two girls who instantly welcome him with open arms.

"Go, CeCe," he says. "We're done."

♪

I DON'T KNOW WHY I'm crying. I have no right to be. I created the situation I am in. I could have asked Holden to leave tonight before anything went as far as it did.

But I didn't.

I start to go back to my room but turn for Thomas's instead. I knock on his door with tears streaming down my face. I don't bother to wipe them away because they are instantly replaced with more.

"Who is it?" he calls out, husky-voiced.

"CeCe," I say, my sobs refusing to stay silent now.

He pulls the door open and stares at me with alarm on his face. "What happened? Are you all right?"

"I think I . . . I might have just ruined everything."

He takes my hand and leads me in the room. "First, clarify everything."

"Barefoot Outlook," I say, the words breaking in half. "The tour."

"Why would you think that?" he asks, pulling me to the bed where we both sink onto the edge of the mattress. "We had a great first show. It couldn't have gone any better."

"It's what happened after the show."

"What?"

I honestly don't know where to start. Finally, I just say, "Holden."

"And you?"

I nod again, miserable.

"Like that hasn't been inevitable," he says.

"Thanks," I say.

"Well, you'd have to be blind not to see it."

"I thought you were my friend."

"I am your friend. Friends tell each other the truth. So what happened, other than you two knocking boots?"

I put my hand over his mouth and say, "We did not knock boots."

He play-wrestles with my hand for a moment and says, "What exactly did you do?"

"I . . . we were kind of headed in that direction," I admit in a low voice, "and Beck walked in."

"Dang," Thomas says, sounding completely serious now. "That's bad."

"He's really angry with me."

"Yeah." He lets out a soft whistle. "Can't say that I blame him."

"He has three naked girls in his room right now, and he's been drinking. That's probably not all."

"Girl," he says, shaking his head, "you sure know how to bring a fella down."

"I didn't mean to," I say, miserable. "I didn't want to hurt him. What happened with Holden tonight wasn't supposed to happen. Oh, Thomas, what if I've messed it all up?"

"Why would you think you've done that?"

"He's pretty mad."

"Beck has as much to gain from Barefoot Outlook hitting it as any of us do. From everything he's said to me, going back to school is the last thing he wants. I doubt he wants to give his dad a reason to say the gig's up."

I shrug. "Maybe."

"Want me to talk to him?"

"I'm not sure it will do any good."

"I think he'll see the logic. But here's my one stipulation," he says, his voice suddenly serious.

I turn my head to look at him. "What?"

"You and Holden cool it until the tour is done."

I want to argue, tell him what happened tonight won't happen again, that we both lost it and things can go back to the way they were. I can't. Because I know that's a lie.

So I nod. Once. Looking down at my hands. "Okay," I say. "Okay."

♪

CeCe

I keep my word to Thomas, but the wear of avoiding both Beck and Holden for three weeks is starting to become evident. I'm not sleeping great, and it's taking more makeup to prevent that fact from showing beneath my eyes.

I've been talking to Mama pretty much every night after the show. We talk about normal things, people back home, who's recently gotten married, had babies, bought a new car, the kind of regular stuff that keeps me from thinking about the strain within our group.

I send her tickets for the Annapolis show, and on the morning she and my Aunt Vera are scheduled to meet me at our hotel, I wake up so excited to see them, I can hardly wait.

I'm standing outside when Aunt Vera's Suburban turns in the parking lot. As soon as she pulls into an open space, I run to the passenger side door, barely waiting for Mama to slide out before throwing my arms around her and hugging her as if I can absorb every ounce of the comfort I know she will fill me with.

"Hello, honey," she says with a catch in her voice, her southern Virginia accent music to my ears. "Gracious, it's good to see you."

I nod and bury my face in her neck. She smells like home, like the bread she makes almost every day and the basil she grows in a pot by the kitchen sink where it gets lots of sun. All of a sudden, I am crying the way I did when I would go to her as a little girl, certain that whatever was wrong, she'd be able to fix.

"Aw, honey, what is it?" she asks, smoothing her hand over the back of my hair.

"Nothing," I say as convincingly as I can manage. "It's just so good to see you."

Late forties looks more like late thirties on her, and I feel proud of her, proud that she is here. She hugs me even tighter, and Aunt Vera waits a couple of minutes before she gets out and hugs me too.

She pulls back and gives me a long look. "Good gracious, child, could you get any prettier?"

I smile a watery smile and say, "You never did go see that eye doctor, did you, Aunt Vera?"

She and Mama both beam at me, and I think not for the first time how much alike they look. They're twins, and a lot of people back home can't tell them apart even though they've known them their whole lives.

I wipe my eyes and say, "It's so good to see you both."

"It's good to see you, honey," Mama says. "We want to hear all about everything you've been doing. So much excitement. I've been telling everybody in town."

"We are so overdue a gabfest," Aunt Vera says.

"There's a Starbucks down the street," I say.

"Perfect," Mama says.

We walk there, Mama and Vera each holding my hand. They set right in on sharing the local gossip. It feels so familiar, so much a part of me that I am deeply homesick. Even so, I feel better already.

♪

"WELL, IT'S NO surprise," Aunt Vera says. "A girl as pretty as you having two boyfriends."

"I don't think that's exactly what she's saying, Vera," Mama says, taking a sip of her house blend.

"Isn't it?" Aunt Vera says, looking at me with a twinkle in her eyes.

"That was never my intention," I say.

"Sometimes, these things just happen. I remember when I was young enough and pretty enough to get myself in such fixes," Aunt Vera says, with the dramatic flair she has been known for my whole life. "Those were the days."

"Hah," Mama says. "Those were the days when you'd go out with the first boy who arrived to pick you up, leaving me to deal with the second one you had then stood up."

I laugh at this image. It's so typical of their relationship. Mama, the responsible one. Vera, leaning on her to right whatever wrongs she happened to ignite.

"So which one are you standing up, my dear?" Aunt Vera says, looking at me over the rim of her Caramel Frappuccino.

"Neither," I say, some of my misery evident in the response.

"You're not seeing either one?" Mama asks, and I can hear that she's worried about me.

I shake my head. "No, but it's fine."

"How can it be fine?" Aunt Vera says with a cluck, cluck. "That's a losing proposition."

"It's complicated," I say.

"So is being unhappy," she adds.

"I'm doing what I've always wanted to do. I have nothing to complain about."

"The heart usually insists on having what it wants," Mama says in her calm, common sense way. "Don't close a door you might later wish you'd left open."

"If only it were that simple, Mama."

"The feeling itself is, honey. Sometimes, we just need to get out of its way."

♪

I SPEND THE rest of the day with them, shopping and laughing at Vera's funny stories about her own dating life. I decide after a point that if I had ever considered taking advice from her, it would have been a bad idea.

On the way back into the hotel, we run into Holden and Thomas in the lobby. I introduce everyone, and we are all polite and friendly. I try not to give Mama or Aunt Vera any clues about my feelings for Holden, but as soon as we step in the elevator, Mama looks at me and says, "It'll be hard for your heart to accept no on that one, honey."

Aunt Vera nods. "Amen to that, sister."

I'd like to offer up at least some token disagreement, but who would I be kidding?

When it's time to leave for the show, Mama and Aunt Vera go with me to my dressing room and help me get ready. It is so wonderful having them there that I know I'm going to miss them terribly once they're gone. We laugh and giggle more like high school best friends than aunt, mother, and daughter. I try to convince Aunt Vera that light blue eye shadow has not yet come back in style. She finally relents but still doesn't agree.

It's only a few minutes before I need to leave the room when a knock sounds at the door. Aunt Vera jogs over to see who it is before I can get there. She pulls it open and then stands there as if she has been lasered to the spot.

"Oh. Good. Day." Aunt Vera utters the words with wide-eyed disbelief. She takes a step back with one hand on her chest.

"Evening, ma'am," Case says, smiling at her with the very same smile that's made his CDs bestsellers.

"Hi, Case," I say. "You might need to take a little pity on Aunt Vera. She's prone to fainting spells."

His grin widens. "I heard you had some beautiful women in here with you tonight. Thought I'd stop by and say hey."

His generosity shouldn't still surprise me, but it does. Especially in light of the fact that I know he must have heard Beck and I aren't seeing each other. "This is my mama, Mira MacKenzie. And her sister, my aunt, Vera Nelson."

"Mira. Vera. Sure is nice to meet you ladies. I can't tell you how much we think of your lovely CeCe here."

"Thank you," Mama says, her smile warm and appreciative. "We think the world of her ourselves."

"I know CeCe got tickets for you tonight but I was hoping y'all might like to use these two from my VIP section. We've created a few perks for special guests, and I'd love for y'all to be a part of it."

"Case," I say. "Thank you. Really."

"Goodness gracious," Aunt Vera says. "Some days you get up and have absolutely no idea what's in store for you."

Case laughs. "I think there's a song lyric in there somewhere, ma'am."

"Be happy to work on that with you," Aunt Vera says.

"That's mighty kind," Case says, smiling. He looks at Mama then, and I notice their gazes linger a moment longer than just polite interest.

Mama glances away first, and I see her cheeks brighten with color. I can't even remember the last time I saw her affected by a man.

"Well," Case says, "I hope y'all enjoy the show."

"I am certain we will," Aunt Vera says.

"Thank you so much," Mama says.

When he's gone, Aunt Vera waits ten seconds or so before she starts to dance around the room. "Did that really happen?"

"That really happened, Vera," Mama says, shaking her head with a smile. "Now settle down before you hurt yourself."

♪

Holden

I'm not sure that I'm old enough to make a conclusion like this yet, but I'm starting to wonder if it's even possible to be completely content in this life.

I should be. In fact, this should be a high point.

We're on the fourth week of our tour, and I don't know that we could have even hoped for the kind of response we've been getting from the crowds in pretty much every city we've visited.

San Diego. Flagstaff. Denver. Omaha. Springfield. Columbus. Annapolis last night. And now tonight in D.C.

We're here for the music. And to get the kind of break we've been given is like winning the hundred million dollar lottery. It almost never happens.

To do anything other than milk every possible moment of enjoyment from this experience makes no sense at all.

Even so, I feel like I'm living in a state of euphoria combined with one of extreme misery. Thomas was right. Staying away from CeCe, with the exception of the time that we're actually rehearsing or performing, is the common sense thing to do. I don't want to blow what we have going with this tour.

It just feels so wrong to put on a show the way we do, smiling, laughing, joking with each other. Beck even manages to pull this off, and I assume that's the power of Thomas's persuasiveness.

As soon as we're off stage though, we go in our separate directions. I've heard there are big name groups who lived like this for years while they played out their contracts; a picture of unity and professionalism when they're on stage, hating each other's guts and not speaking when they're off. That doesn't make me feel any better.

If I could rewind to that night in CeCe's dressing room and push pause for everything that I wanted to happen between us, I would. We should all be hanging out together, seeing as much of the towns we're in as we can, but unless I go somewhere with Thomas, I'm alone. The same is true for CeCe. Which means we both spend a lot of time by ourselves.

I'm just getting out of the shower when I hear a knock on the door of my hotel room. I wrap a towel around my waist and answer it.

Thomas is standing in the hall, wearing an enormous Stetson and new cowboy boots. I lean back and give him an appraising look.

"You've been shopping," I say.

"Fruits of my labor," he says. "We've got the whole day to tour the city before we need to be at the arena. I thought you and me and CeCe could see what there is to see."

I wave him in. "Aren't you the one who grounded us from being together?"

"I'll be the chaperone."

"I don't know, Thomas. I doubt that CeCe would–"

"I already asked her. She said yes."

I can't hide my surprise when I say, "Oh."

"Well? Get your britches on then."

"It seems like it'll be awkward."

"Probably will since you two have trouble keeping your hands off each other. I'll sit between you."

I roll my eyes. "What about Beck?"

"He, apparently, has a date."

I should feel glad about this but I wonder if it hurts CeCe that he's obviously not wasting any time in moving on. "Where are we going?"

"Where else? To hear some music."

♪

WE WALK THE half mile or so from our hotel to the festival in downtown D.C. Thomas keeps his word and walks in between CeCe and me. We both pretend not to notice. I can't stop myself from stealing glimpses of her out of the corner of my eye. She's wearing an orange skirt and a pink tank top. She looks like she's upped her running because her arms are even leaner and more cut than they were at the beginning of the tour.

"Bark-Fest is a fundraiser for a local No-Kill rescue," Thomas says. "Sounds like they raise a boatload of money every year."

"That's great," CeCe says, but she looks distracted, as if her thoughts are somewhere else.

We've arrived at the concession area. Tents and booths are set up all around us, and the smell of funnel cakes and cotton candy permeates the air.

"I need a Coke," Thomas says, pointing at a stand not too far away. "Anybody want one?"

"I'm good," I say.

"No, thanks," CeCe says.

"Be right back," Thomas says.

"I thought he was going to stay between us," I say, the words out before I think to stop them.

A small smile touches the corners of CeCe's mouth. "He did say that, didn't he?"

I turn to let myself look at her. It's only then that I realize I haven't been looking at her full on but turning away whenever I started to take in too much of her. Our gazes catch, and we stare at each other for several long moments.

"How are you?" I ask, the question soft, tentative.

"I'm okay," she says. "Are you?"

I start to answer with something off-hand, but I can't make myself be flip. "Sometimes. The other times? Not so much."

"Kind of a mess, isn't it?" CeCe says.

"I'm sorry for what happened that night. Beck walking in and everything."

"I'm not," she says.

I don't know how to respond to this so I say, "What do you mean?"

"I'm not sorry for what happened between us. I never wanted to hurt Beck, but I'm not sorry for the way I feel about you."

"CeCe," I say, with no idea of where to go from here. I want to pull her to me and kiss her with every drop of need inside me. I'm just about to give in and do exactly that when my phone buzzes. CeCe's makes its text alert sound a second later.

I glance at the screen, see it's from Thomas.

She looks at hers. "Thomas."

We read the message at the same time.

Sorry for the deception, but tired of watching you be miserable. No more middle man. Find your way wherever you need to go. Love you both.

When we're done, we look at each other as if we're not sure what to make of it.

"But why would he change his mind?"

I shake my head. "I don't know."

We stand there for what feels like a very long time. I hold out my hand. CeCe takes it.

CeCe

Holden tugboats me through the crowd, weaving and winding until we reach the edge of the festival and a high stonewall. He pulls me behind it so that we are virtually hidden from anyone passing by.

He presses me against it, one hand on each of my shoulders, looking down at me with the fiercest need I have ever seen in anyone's eyes.

It is an exact reflection of what I feel. And suddenly, I don't want to ignore it any longer. I don't want to turn away from the constant buzz of need inside me, whether I'm next to him or nowhere near. It's there when I wake up in the morning. When I go to sleep at night. No matter what I do to pretend it isn't, it never leaves. Never stops. Instead, it just continues to grow like a storm building way out in the ocean, increasing in power until there is no denying its existence, its inevitable crash into shore.

I reach for him then, cup my hand at the back of his neck and pull him in. He comes to me with an urgency that tells me he has simply been waiting for the invitation. His mouth is on mine in full assault, full surrender. I kiss him with a need I have never in my life known. All this time of denying, subduing, turning away from. I think I will surely drown in its sudden pent-up release.

He lifts me and sets me on the stone wall, stepping in between my legs and bringing us as close as it is physically possible to be in broad daylight in a public place.

I lock my arms around his waist, and we kiss each other as if we are living out our last moments on earth, almost out of time.

"CeCe." My name is ragged on his lips, and I touch his mouth, wanting to feel him say it.

"Is this real?" I ask.

"Nothing in my life has ever felt as real as you," he says. "If I don't get you somewhere alone, I think I might actually stop breathing."

I want to smile, laugh, make light of what he's just said, but I can't because I feel the very same way. "Where?" I ask in little more than a whisper.

He lifts me off the wall and, clasping my hand in his, starts pulling me down the street at a near run.

I should protest, tell him this is crazy, that we need to stop, go back. For the life of me, I cannot make myself do anything other than hold onto him and follow.

In less than five minutes, we slow to a walk just before the entrance to a very luxurious hotel front. A discreet sign says **The Montgomery Mansion.**

I remember reading about it in a magazine once. I stop suddenly and pull on Holden's hand, protesting, "We can't go here. It's a five-star hotel."

"I want to see you naked on five-star sheets."

The words send a ripple of heat through me.

That's crazy. We have to go back. Any of these responses would have been appropriate. But that's not what comes out.

"Do I get to see *you* on those sheets?" I ask.

He doesn't answer but propels me forward through the main door of the hotel and doesn't stop until we reach the front desk.

An older man with white hair and smart-looking spectacles glances up at us with a welcoming smile. "Good morning. Welcome to the Montgomery Mansion. How may I help you?"

"We'd like a room, please," Holden says.

"Do you have a reservation, sir?"

"No, we don't."

I feel my face turn four different shades of red, one layered over the other. I squeeze Holden's hand in an attempt to convey that we should leave and forget about this.

But the man smiles and says, "Let me see what I can do."

He taps on the keyboard in front of him for a minute or more before looking up and saying, "Ah, yes. We do have something available for you." He states the rate, and I blink at the amount.

Holden hands him a credit card. "We'll take that."

"Very good, sir." The man runs the card and gives it back to Holden along with a room key. "Do you have any bags we can help you with?" His expression remains neutral in the manner of someone who is expected to be discreet.

"No, thank you," Holden says.

"Enjoy your day then," the man says, nodding as we turn to leave.

Once we're alone in the elevator, Holden walks me back against one wall and begins kissing me again. I can't stop myself from kissing him, even though my cheeks are still burning from the front desk experience.

Just as the elevator dings, I say, "Like he didn't know why we wanted a room."

Holden smiles against my mouth. "Do you think we're the first?"

"That doesn't make it any less embarrassing."

"Embarrassed is the very last thing I'm feeling right now," he says, taking my hand and leading me down the long hallway.

"How many months' rent did you just spend?" I ask, breathless.

We're at the door now. He leans in. "Stop talking so I can kiss you."

I do, and he does. So slowly and thoroughly that my legs weaken beneath me, and I lean into him, not sure of anything except that I want more.

He opens the door, walks us backwards inside, and kicks it closed behind us. From there, he swoops me up as if I weigh nothing. I loop my arms around his neck and kiss him with every ounce of feeling I have for him.

When he reaches the side of the bed, he lets go of my legs and I slide to the floor.

He stares down at me with the most intense seriousness I've ever seen in him. "I wake up in the morning, and you're my first thought," he says. "When I go to bed at night, it's your voice I hear right before I fall asleep. I've tried to make myself forget you as anything other than a friend. I can't. And I can't imagine my life meaning anything near what it would mean if you're part of it."

Tears well in my eyes, and I try to blink them back, but it doesn't work. "I love you, Holden."

"I love you, baby. So much."

We fall onto the bed together, arms wrapped tight around one another. And absolutely everything ceases to exist except this need we have for each other.

I unbutton his shirt, slide it from his shoulders and wait for him to shrug out of it. I run my hand across the muscled contours of his chest then down the curve of his left bicep.

"Do you have any idea how beautiful you are?" I ask him.

He gives me a very heated look that makes me want to wrap myself around him and never let go.

"You're the one who's beautiful," he says.

"No, I mean it," I say, tracing one finger down the center of his well-honed abs. "Beautiful like art that I just want to stare at for as long as it takes to absorb every inch of what I see."

"CeCe," he starts, but I stop him with a kiss that goes on for quite some time, a slow dance of exploration, of longing, of pleasure.

Holden drops his head back when my lips find his neck. He makes a sound of need that I want to satisfy in every way I possibly can.

He rolls me over then, settles his long body onto mine and lifts my shirt over my head, pulling it off and tossing it onto the floor.

It is the first time we've been against each other this way, skin to skin, and I feel as if I've been ignited deep inside with a heat so consuming that only he will be able to direct it in a way that does not turn me to vapor.

And we keep kissing. Long, slow, full, deep kisses that both fill me up and drain me. I want to give him everything. Be everything he needs. But I am suddenly swamped with a wave of uncertainty. I have no idea how to tell him I've never done this before.

I press a hand to his chest and say his name.

He lifts up to look down at me through eyes hazed with want. "What is it?" he asks, his voice soft and husky.

"Holden . . . I haven't been with . . . I've never done this before."

He goes completely still above me. I watch his face as he processes what I have just said. When comprehension fully registers, he rolls across the bed and lies flat on his back, staring at the ceiling and breathing hard.

"You've. . . never. . . been with anyone?"

I shake my head, feeling something well beyond embarrassed

now. We lie there like that for a good bit while I wish I could blink and disappear.

Finally, Holden turns over on his side, rising up on one elbow to stare into my eyes. "CeCe?"

"What?" I ask without looking at him, feeling the heat in my face.

"Look at me," he says gently.

I turn my head, slowly, finally letting myself meet his gaze.

He reaches out and touches my cheek. "I'm glad you told me. I want this to be different," he says. "I want us to be different."

"What do you mean?" I ask, my stomach suddenly tight with worry that he will say this is a mistake.

"This isn't casual. And it never could be."

I nod once. "I know."

"I love you, CeCe. I want to be with you. Not just here and now, but every single day of my life. Every single night of my life."

Relieved beyond words, I smile and lace my fingers through his. "I want to be with you."

"Then let's make it forever," he says, taking my hand in his. "CeCe MacKenzie, will you marry me?"

I have to wonder if I've actually heard him say this or if I have imagined it. "Do you mean it?" I ask in little more than a whisper.

He loops an arm around my waist and pulls me up close until we are touching, skin to skin. "I've never meant anything more in my life."

Tears well in my eyes, seep out and slip down my cheeks. I wipe them away with the back of my hand. "Then, yes," I say. "Yes. Yes. Yes."

♪

CeCe

Case's Fan Appreciation party is wide open by the time I change into jeans and a tank top and make my way to the big white tent set up alongside two of the tour buses. I feel lit up inside with the secret I have yet to share with anyone. Holden wants to tell Thomas after the show tonight. And I am going to tell Beck. As painful as it will be, I have to tell him.

Music is blasting from two enormous stage speakers. I don't recognize hardly anyone at first, but then I spot Thomas and Beck standing next to a table loaded with trays of sandwiches and platters of fruit and cookies.

My stomach drops and I feel sick at the thought of hurting Beck. I have to be honest with him. I owe him that.

Thomas spots me and waves me over, taking my hand and pulling me in to kiss me on the cheek. "What a show. You were amazing out there tonight."

"Everyone was," I say, letting myself glance at Beck then. "I thought it was our best of the tour."

Beck nods, but doesn't answer. "Can we talk, Beck?" I ask, my heart pounding so hard I know he can hear it.

"Yeah," he says.

Thomas looks at both of us with compassion in his eyes. "Y'all go easy on each other, okay?"

And with that he walks away, stopping to talk with some of the crew where they are loading plates with sandwiches.

"Are we doing this here?" Beck asks.

"I'd rather go somewhere else," I say.

Just then Case comes in and waves for everyone's attention. The dull roar of conversation lowers and succumbs to silence.

"Thanks y'all," Case says. "I hope everyone's having a good time. You've sure earned it. I can honestly say that so far this is the best tour I've ever been a part of. I want to thank each of you for the role you played in making it happen. It's no accident that it's a success. And without the stellar fans who are celebrating with us here tonight, none of this would be possible."

Cheers start in a wave and crescendo with whistles and clapping. Someone yells out, "You rock, Case!"

Shouts of agreement follow. He raises a hand, smiling and waiting for the volume to lower to a level where he can be heard. "Thank you, again. Every one of you."

Someone starts opening Champagne and several toasts are made by Rhys, Case's producer and a few of the band members.

My eyes are drawn to a tall figure standing at the edge of the tent. The white-blonde short-cropped hair triggers instant recognition. It's the guy from our first concert in San Diego.

He walks over to one of the tables now, picks up a plate, a couple of sandwiches, steps back and starts eating.

I should let someone know the guy is here. But what am I going to say? He was mean to me and he shouldn't be here?

I'm trying to decide what to do when Case waves Beck forward.

"Come on up here, son," he calls out. "Thomas, Holden, CeCe, y'all too!"

We walk through the crowd of people to the center of the tent where Case is waiting. Holden and Thomas thread their way in, standing on one side of Case, Beck and I on the other.

"I just want to say how proud I am of these four," Case says. "They had about three weeks to put together what you've seen them do during this tour. It's clear from the way all you fans have responded to them, you'll be seeing a lot more of them."

Whistles and clapping follow. Case hands the microphone to Thomas and asks, "Anything y'all want to say?"

Thomas clears his throat and then, "Thank you for the opportunity, Case. I'm not sure we could ever do justice with words our appreciation for the shot you've given us. And how much I admire you for who you are and what you do. You live your life by paying it forward, and if I ever get the chance to do for someone else what you've done for us, I hope I'll be as generous."

"You could start by paying it forward with me," a voice calls out from the guests. "Jared Ryner."

The name rings out in the otherwise silent tent. I look into the crowd and see that it came from the blonde guy from San Diego. My heart starts to pound so hard that I can feel it against my chest.

He drops the now empty plate onto the table, wipes his hands on his jeans. "Do you know how many years I spent in Nashville trying to get someone to give me a shot?"

People start to shift where they stand, uncomfortable and unsure of where this is going.

"Eight," he says. "Eight years. Playing on street corners. Exit ramps off the interstate. Knocking on doors. Sending songs to record companies and never getting a call back."

People are now starting to back away from the center of the tent, as if they all sense that something's not quite right.

Somebody calls out, "Are you supposed to be here, Jared?"

The guy laughs then, as if something hysterically funny has just been said. "No," he says, trying to catch his breath. "I suppose that's the punch line to my eight years of working to get a break. I never actually belonged. There must have been some secret pass code no one ever bothered to let me in on."

Another man's voice rings out with authority, "Someone call Security and get him out of here."

But Jared lifts the front of his shirt and pulls a handgun from the waist of his jeans. "I'm afraid it's a little late for that," he says, raising it up and firing it once through the top of the tent.

Screams erupt and people start to push and shove to get out. He points the gun at the center of the crowd and fires again. A man in a white shirt standing a few yards away from us tilts forward and then collapses onto the ground, blood spilling from his neck like water from a hose.

All around, women begin screaming. I am frozen where I stand. Holden steps in front of me and calls out, "Jared! Man, this isn't the way. Put the gun down, and let's go outside and talk."

He looks at Holden and laughs. "Talk with you? The big hottie on stage? What would you and I have to talk about? No matter how good my music is, I'm never going to get the same chances as a guy who looks like you. How is that fair?"

"A man may die because of you," Holden says, his voice calm and even. "That's the next pressing thing on your list. You still have a chance to turn this around if you want to."

"There's no turning anything around now. It took me a while but I finally figured that out."

I hear the wail of sirens in the distance. Holden steps back and presses against me, his body fully blocking me from seeing where Jared is or what he's doing.

Case moves away from us and walks toward him. "Son. Come on. Put the gun down. You've taken this far enough."

"I suggest you stop right there," he says, pointing the weapon at Case.

Case raises his hands, saying, "Like Holden said, let's go outside and see if we can work this out."

"Don't you see, Mr. Country Music Star," he says, sarcasm underlining every word, "I've already got it worked out. Eye for an eye and all that. If I don't get my dream, then it seems right that I cancel a few others on my way out. Am I the only one that makes sense to?"

Beck reaches out and grabs his dad, pulling him back to where we're standing. "Get out of here, man! The police will be here any second."

The sirens scream like they're right outside the tent now. Car doors slam. I hear the sound of running. I step out from behind Holden and scream, "Go! Just go! End this now!"

Jared Ryner has a look on his face that I've never seen on the face of another human being. He's not leaving this world alone. His eyes say it as clearly as if I have heard him speak the words.

It happens so fast there's no time to say anything else, to move, or to run. He lifts the gun, fires, and Thomas slumps forward, then drops to the ground. I hear myself screaming, a wail I don't even recognize.

Another shot, and Case goes down, falling backwards into the people standing behind us. The next shot takes Beck. He staggers and slumps to the ground next to his dad.

It is surreal now. None of this can be happening. I feel the bullet enter my body with the realization that I have been hit, only I have no idea where. My body is instantly infused with white-hot pain, and

I drop to my knees. I hear a roar of fury, and realize that it has come from Holden. He is charging the guy, but the gun is lifting and I know what is coming. I hear my scream as if I am a million miles from it. I feel the earth tremble with my fury as Holden stops with the bullet's impact. He stands for a moment, sways and then collapses.

Police are rushing into the tent, an entire force of them. Panic has taken over, and the screaming I now hear is not my own. I try to get up, lifting myself on one elbow. My face is wet, and I'm not sure if it's with tears or blood.

I see the policeman body tackle the shooter, taking him down, down, down, but not in time to prevent Jared Ryner from putting the gun to his temple and pulling the trigger.

♪

Nashville - Book Four - Pleasure in the Rain

THE NASHVILLE SERIES
BOOK FOUR

pleasure
in the
rain

RITA® AWARD WINNING AUTHOR
INGLATH
COOPER

Books by Inglath Cooper

My Italian Lover – What If – Book One
Fences
Dragonfly Summer – Book Two – Smith Mountain Lake Series
Blue Wide Sky – Book One – Smith Mountain Lake Series
That Month in Tuscany
Crossing Tinker's Knob
Jane Austen Girl
Good Guys Love Dogs
Truths and Roses
Nashville – Book Ten – Not Without You
Nashville – Book Nine – You, Me and a Palm Tree
Nashville – Book Eight – R U Serious
Nashville – Book Seven – Commit
Nashville – Book Six – Sweet Tea and Me
Nashville – Book Five – Amazed
Nashville – Book Four – Pleasure in the Rain
Nashville – Book Three – What We Feel
Nashville – Book Two – Hammer and a Song
Nashville – Book One – Ready to Reach
On Angel's Wings
A Gift of Grace
RITA® Award Winner John Riley's Girl
A Woman With Secrets
Unfinished Business
A Woman Like Annie
The Lost Daughter of Pigeon Hollow
A Year and a Day

Dear Reader,

I would like to thank you for taking the time to read my story. There are so many wonderful books to choose from these days, and I am hugely appreciative that you chose mine.

If you'd like to try another of my books – Good Guys Love Dogs – for FREE, please click here.

Please join my mailing list for updates on new releases and giveaways! Just go to http://www.inglathcooper.com – come check out my Facebook page for postings on books, dogs and things that make life good!

Wishing you many, many happy afternoons of reading pleasure.

All best,

Inglath

About Inglath Cooper

RITA® Award-winning author Inglath Cooper was born in Virginia. She is a graduate of Virginia Tech with a degree in English. She fell in love with books as soon as she learned how to read. "My mom read to us before bed, and I think that's how I started to love stories. It was like a little mini-vacation we looked forward to every night before going to sleep. I think I eventually read most of the books in my elementary school library."

That love for books translated into a natural love for writing and a desire to create stories that other readers could get lost in, just as she had gotten lost in her favorite books. Her stories focus on the dynamics of relationships, those between a man and a woman, mother and daughter, sisters, friends. They most often take place in small Virginia towns very much like the one where she grew up and are peopled with characters who reflect those values and traditions.

"There's something about small-town life that's just part of who I am. I've had the desire to live in other places, wondered what it would be like to be a true Manhattanite, but the thing I know I would miss is the familiarity of faces everywhere I go. There's a lot to be said for going in the grocery store and seeing ten people you know!"

Inglath Cooper is an avid supporter of companion animal rescue and is a volunteer and donor for the Franklin County Humane Society. She and her family have fostered many dogs and cats that have gone on to be adopted by other families. "The rewards are endless. It's an eye-opening moment to realize that what one person throws away can fill another person's life with love and joy."

Follow Inglath on Facebook

at www.facebook.com/inglathcooperbooks

Join her mailing list for news of new releases and giveaways at www.inglathcooper.com

Made in the USA
Columbia, SC
18 May 2020